VIOLET AMONG THIEVES

AJ WYNN

This is a work of fiction. All names, characters, places, and incidents are a product of the author's imagination or are used fictitiously. Any resemblance to actual persons, living or dead, events, or locations is entirely coincidental.

No part of this work was generated using artificial intelligence or large language models. All content was written solely by the author.

First paperback edition October 2026

Cover designed by: Rachel McEwan Designs
Edited by: Sam Willow
Proofread by: EF Watson
Cliffhaven floorplans by: Termeh Studios
Author illustration by: Bugdrawstuff

Ebook ISBN: 979-8-9895960-6-5
Paperback ISBN: 979-8-9895960-7-2

www.AJWynn.com

Formatted with Vellum

Violet Among Thieves

AJ WYNN

AUTHOR'S NOTE

Violet Among Thieves is a cozy locked room mystery romance novella with spice, following an established couple.

It can be read as a standalone but will be **greatly enhanced** if preceded by *The Other Side* and *Last Chance Christmas.*

May you find your happily ever after,

along with Chance & Violet.

♡aj

CLIFFHAVEN

MENDOCINO, CA

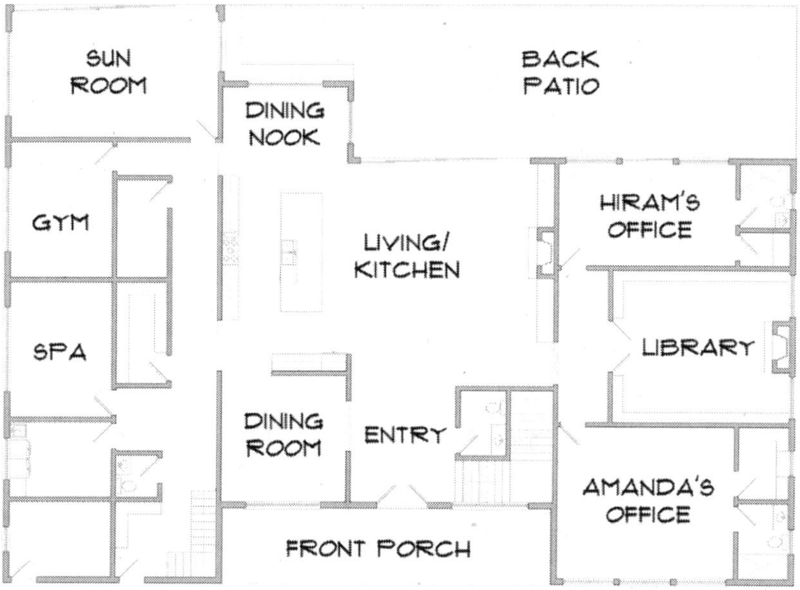

FLOORPLAN CREATED BY
TERMEH STUDIOS

PROLOGUE

"It has to be a mistake," she sobbed into Hiram's chest. "They can't be gone. They're all I had left of her." I knew she meant her grandmother.

"What happened?" Chance asked, looking between me and Amanda.

"The safe's empty," I told him. "Someone took all of Amanda's jewelry—your grandma's pieces."

His lips parted in surprise.

"It's all priceless—irreplaceable," Amanda cried.

All the color had drained from Chance's face. "That's not—but we were here—everything was there last night," he stuttered before pacing over to the walk-in closet.

I was hot on Chance's heels, watching as he swung open the safe and turned to me, absolutely stunned. "How did this happen?"

I shook my head, still in shock myself.

He pushed past me, walking back into the bedroom. "We need to call the police right now."

"The lines are down." Hiram's jaw ticked.

"Don't you have a satellite phone or a ham radio or something?" Chance said frantically.

Hiram pursed his lips while Amanda continued to cry on his shoulder.

"Who would do this?" She hiccupped.

Who indeed.

1

CHANCE

"Would you marry me tomorrow?" I whispered.

"I'd marry you today," Violet replied softly, the sweetest smile curling her lips as she regarded me with all the love and devotion I still had trouble accepting I was deserving of.

What had started as a joke between us shortly after our engagement had become an intimate way for us to check in with each other.

She was nestled into the bed, a breath away from me, barely having awoken from sleep, and it was those exact moments that I perhaps cherished the most. The heartbeats between breaths in which both of us laid ourselves bare to each other, exposing every bit of vulnerable flesh, waiting, and hoping, to be embraced instead of turned away. We had yet to fail one another, and I'd never needed someone the way I needed Violet.

"What kind of wedding do you want?" I asked. I'd posed the question to her before.

Often she joked with outlandish requests of gothic castles or only animal guests, but that day, she looked introspective as she replied with what felt like a more authentic response, building upon the brief bits she'd shared with me in the last few months, since she'd accepted my proposal.

"Small," she said quietly, reaching her hand out to twine her fingers with mine, between us in the bed. "Just us."

I wasn't surprised to hear it. The thought of Violet ever agreeing to some grand event would have made me chuckle. So small it would be. I nodded in agreement, encouraging her to continue.

"Maybe by the ocean." She bit her bottom lip while her mind likely continued to whirl. "I bet your mom knows some nice places in Portland that would work."

"And what will you be wearing?" I nestled closer to her, enjoying the way the early rays of dawn illuminated her face, making her green eyes seem so bright and fathomless.

"Something simple." She squinted, as if she couldn't quite

imagine what it would look like. "I might need Amanda's help," Violet admitted.

I inched forward, placing a soft kiss on the tip of her nose. "What should I wear?"

"Your charcoal suit." She sighed immediately, as if she'd envisioned me at the wedding more than she'd thought of herself. "With the light blue tie that brings out your eyes." Her smile deepened as her eyes focused on mine. "You look so handsome in that suit."

I felt a blush sweep across my cheeks at the compliment. Anytime I wore that suit (usually saved for donor events at the school), she'd inevitably mention how she felt about it, and if I was lucky, it would lead to her divesting me of each article piece by piece, at the end of the day.

"Thank you, muse." I squeezed her hand. "And what will your vows be?"

"I can't spoil them." She reeled back. "You'll just have to wait and see." We shared a conspiratorial smirk at the thought.

Looking at her across from me, so soft and open, I felt a pang of guilt. I never liked keeping things from Violet. Once I'd broken through her hard exterior, her love flowed so freely, it often overwhelmed me with her open devotion.

I wasn't sure I was worthy of such affection, but she made me want to be a better man. I was determined to be enough for her. And there was no room for secrets between us, but I did my best to justify the things I'd been keeping to myself the last few weeks, and I just had to hope she'd forgive me when she discovered the truth.

I opened my mouth, a confession almost slipping from my lips, but a scratch and a whine at the bedroom door cut me off before I had the chance.

Violet's eyes lit up at the sound before she slipped from the bed to open the door and let Toby come into the room. He bounded up into the bed, his wet nose burrowing into my neck as he snuggled under the covers, eventually retreating to Violet when she was back in the bed.

"My baby..." she crooned as she cuddled his soft little body against hers.

I loved watching her with the little dog I'd surprised her with two months prior. From the moment I'd laid eyes on him, I'd known he was for her...for us. And that adorable little terrier mutt, with his brindle-colored fur and big brown eyes, had immediately become the missing piece neither of us had known we'd needed to make our own little family.

"I don't want to leave him," Violet whined, her gaze bouncing from Toby back up to me.

"We'll only be gone a few days, and you know how excited Mrs. Elwood is to watch him. She told me she pulled all of her old dog's beds and toys out from the basement." I reached out to tuck a stray strand of hair behind Violet's ear.

My sister, Amanda, had invited us to spend spring break with her and Hiram in California at their new home, dubbed Cliffhaven. It boasted a beautiful coastal view, impeccable amenities, and she'd been talking nonstop about all the architectural details.

"But he's just a baby." Violet pouted. "What if he forgets us?"

Despite Violet calling Toby a baby or a puppy, the vet believed he was around three years old. "He could never forget you, sweetheart," I promised, knowing her hesitance was just nervousness for the flight. My beautiful fiancée had never been on a plane before, and her anxiety had been through the roof the last week as the reality of our travel set in. "You don't want to disappoint Amanda, do you?" I smiled, teasing her. "She probably has rooms full of clothes for you."

Violet managed to wince and chuckle at the same time at the thought.

"Let's get you some coffee and let him outside and you'll feel better." I scratched behind Toby's ears, earning his attention for a brief moment. Although I'd met the little dog first, he'd belonged to Violet from the second he'd laid eyes on her.

"Okay," she reluctantly agreed, sitting up in the bed, "But I might cry when I drop him off."

I leaned forward, placing a soft kiss on her lips. "It'll be worth it," I assured her.

"I think you've packed too much, muse." I laughed, staring at her mostly empty small hardback carry-on case, sitting open on the bench at the end of the bed.

"I know you were joking about Amanda having clothes for me, but we both know she will, so what's the point of packing when whatever I bring will be useless?" She frowned, sitting down next to my suitcase on the side of the bed.

"You should bring stuff you're comfortable in." I reached out, running my fingers through her hair before hooking my finger under her chin and tilting up her face to look at me.

"I just want you to be able to relax. Amanda means well, but if you want to lounge around in pajama pants and one of my hoodies, then that's what you should do." I leaned down and placed a soft kiss on her lips, relishing the way her eyes fluttered closed and how quickly her body canted toward mine.

"Thank you, Chance," she whispered as she pulled away.

I watched the sway of her hips as she went over to her dresser to sort through her pajamas, and pulled out the soft black pair she'd been favoring as of late. When she returned to her suitcase and gently slipped them inside, her big eyes peered up at me. I raised an eyebrow, waiting for her question. "I can take one of your hoodies?" she asked shyly.

"Whatever ones you want." I grinned. I loved seeing her in my clothes. And the best part was that they smelled like her after she returned them.

"Okay." She beamed, making her way toward the closet to dig through my clothes.

Her nerves were only briefly calmed because she had something else to focus on, but I knew the moment the packing was over, they'd return. I would comfort her the best way I knew how, but it was up to Violet to work through her emotions.

I continued to tuck my things away in my suitcase as she puttered around the house, unsure of what to bring, as she'd never really done any sort of traveling before.

I chuckled to myself, thinking how out of whack our routine had been this morning, as I'd gotten used to the comfort and permanence of the habits we'd developed. I always got coffee ready in the morning and Violet took care of Toby. We split chores and meals. I tried my best to keep things as even as possible, even with the mental load.

Sometimes it was hard to wrestle tasks back from Violet, as she was so used to taking care of others around her, as well as herself, she'd never stopped to think about the fact that she could ask for help. She still didn't ask. And I'd gotten to a point where I didn't even offer anymore, I just did things I knew she needed, which always left her stunned, much to my amusement.

If I was honest with myself, it was just as much about showing her how much I loved her through my actions, not just words, as it was doing everything in my power to keep her. Growing up, it always felt like love seemed to have rules I was never aware of, always feeling left behind and wondering why I wasn't worthy of my father's admiration, or my mother's time instead of her charities. As an adult, I understood they had done their best, but the results lingered.

Pursuing Violet had been such a rush, but was nothing compared to how her unconditional love felt. It was like nothing else I'd ever experienced before, or would ever experience again. She couldn't help but love me with all her heart, which made it all the easier to love her in the same way.

Loving Violet made me want things I'd spent most of my life pretending I didn't deserve. I didn't want to feel unworthy of her, and she'd be horrified if she knew I worried about her feelings at all, but she was everything to me, and she'd been let down by everyone else she'd cared about. I couldn't stomach the thought of disappointing her. So I focused on what I could control, which was showing up for her every single day, remaining open to her, and cherishing her like there might not be another tomorrow.

When Violet took her seat in the airport taxi, teary-eyed, after dropping off Toby with our next-door neighbor, I pulled her into my arms and kissed away her tears. "I know it's silly. I know he'll be okay." She sniffled.

"It's not silly," I told her, massaging my thumb into the base of her neck to get her to relax against me. I adored how much she loved that little dog. I was enamored with the little family we were building.

I almost told her then what I had been keeping from her, but she'd find out soon enough, and I knew it would be worth the wait.

2

VIOLET

"He missed the airport exit," I grumbled quietly to Chance in the back seat of the cab.

Chance just smiled. "It'll be okay. We'll get there. We've got plenty of time."

I narrowed my eyes at him. He'd been acting off for the last few weeks...worried almost. It wasn't like him, and it didn't make sense that he'd be nervous for this trip. We were practically attached at the hip when we weren't teaching, and we were close with Amanda and Hiram. He shouldn't have had anything to worry about...except maybe *me*...

I looked up at Chance, suddenly realizing maybe his anxious energy was because he was nervous for me, for this flight, for the trip. He always wanted everything to go perfectly. He constantly went out of his way to make things easier for me.

For a moment, guilt swamped me that my usually happy-go-lucky boyfriend, now fiancé (still felt weird), was worried I wouldn't enjoy myself on a trip we'd been looking forward to for weeks.

"I love you," I told him, pressing a kiss to the edge of his jaw.

"I love you too, sweetheart." He rested his cheek against the top of my head, pulling me into his side.

Turning my attention back to the narrow access road the driver had surely taken by mistake, I noticed the taxi was slowing to a stop at a gate, with signs noting that it was a private entrance.

"Are we going to get in trouble for going to the wrong entrance?" I whispered to Chance nervously.

"We're in the right place," he assured me.

"But it says private." I pointed to the sign.

"It's okay." He squeezed my hand.

And sure enough, the security officer waved the car through after the driver handed him something. Brow furrowed, I watched through the window as we made our way past hangars, warehouses, and buildings, to an indiscreet, small office building that was all windows and clean lines.

"Where are we?" I asked Chance as he was sliding out of his side of the car.

But before he could answer, the driver had made it around my side to open my door for me. I swallowed the lump in my throat. I felt silly for not having been on a plane before. But growing up, my mom could barely afford to keep the utilities in the house running, let alone get us plane tickets to some far-flung vacation.

When I'd dated Harry Ainsworth, a well-to-do trust fund kid I'd met in college, he'd always talk about going on vacations together, but somehow ended up going with friends and leaving me behind with my nose buried in books, trying to take advantage of every moment of college I had.

However, I'd watched enough TV shows and movies to know this wasn't a regular airport. And, sure, the Portland airport was smaller, but this wasn't right.

"Chance?" I met his eyes, nervousness evident in my voice as he rounded the car to take my hand. "What about our bags?" I glanced at the driver and another worker who had just come out of the building we were parked in front of to take our luggage from the trunk.

"You just need your purse. They'll take care of the rest." He squeezed my hand before slipping each of the men folded bills and then turning to escort me inside.

"Good afternoon, Mr. and Mrs. Harper," a woman greeted us with a warm smile the moment we entered the lobby of the small building. It smelled like a mixture of jet fuel and coffee, with plush carpet and multiple leather chairs and sofas overlooking a large window that offered a full view of the tarmac.

I blinked, having just digested what the woman had called us. I'd decided I would never be Mrs. Harper, as I was far too attached to my maiden name, Price, which came from the father who had died before I was born, but to whom I felt a very strong connection, nonetheless. Chance wasn't at all bothered by the request when I'd explained my feelings on the matter late one night, shortly after our engagement. Still, I found that I didn't mind being tied to him in name, so I didn't correct the woman.

"Your plane is ready for you, but feel free to use the facilities or help yourself to the food and coffee we have available before your departure." She motioned toward a small kitchenette that had a small but fancy-looking display of snacks and treats, along with an expensive coffee machine that reflected the bright overhead lighting on the chrome dials and panels.

"I'll get you a latte while you use the bathroom." Chance corralled me toward the restroom door.

I opened my mouth to reply, but the words didn't come. All I could think was that this wasn't at all what I had expected. I trusted Chance that we were where he'd intended us to be, but it didn't make sense. Maybe he thought getting us a private gate would make me less nervous, and it was nice not having to deal with crowds or TSA, which had been one of my larger concerns, but I felt like I was still missing something.

"Here you go." Chance handed me a warm coffee cup when I returned to the office. "I had them pack up some of the food for us and we can eat it on the plane if you're hungry. I know Amanda has a late dinner planned for us, but you didn't eat much for breakfast."

I just stared at him.

The attendant approached, asking us to follow her outside. The cold air hit my face like a wall, and even though it wasn't supposed to be balmy in Northern California in March, I thought anything would be better than the bone-deep chill of a Maine winter.

When we turned the corner of the building, I saw what I'd been missing: a small private jet sat neatly on the tarmac with a narrow staircase extended from the door.

"All your luggage has been loaded, and they'll take off as soon as you're settled," the attendant assured us as we walked toward the stairs.

"Chance?" I stared up at him. "You did this?"

"Amanda." He smiled down at me. "When she found out it was your first time on a plane, she insisted."

I didn't know how to feel. I was overwhelmed with the privilege, but felt completely unprepared and unworthy for something that I never could have dreamt of for myself.

"Did you take the Dramamine, like I suggested?" he asked as we made our way up the stairs.

"Yes," I replied, eyes wide as I took in the small cabin with camel-colored leather seats just beyond a seating area for the flight attendant that awaited us with a smile. There were two pairs facing each other, like on a train, and behind them, on one side, two seats faced each other with a table in between, and across from it was a couch that could sit perhaps three passengers.

"Let's sit together." Chance motioned toward the couch at the back of the plane. His tall frame was bent over in the small cabin, reminding me of how large he was compared to my slight stature, as I was just short enough to be able to stand at my full height.

I made my way forward, sitting down where he'd instructed, still feeling shocked by this turn of events. I watched as Chance helped me buckle in, and found I couldn't focus while the flight attendant let us know about safety procedures and where the plane's amenities were located.

"It might be a little bumpy on take-off and landing because it's a smaller plane," Chance told me after the attendant had retreated to her seat, pulling closed the partition that separated her from the rest of the plane. "But I promise it'll be okay."

Bumpy was a bit of an understatement, compared to what I was expecting, but Chance was kind enough to let me cling to him, and I was glad he'd chosen these seats, so I could focus on the warmth of his body, the smell of his aftershave, and the softness of his sweater against my cheek.

But once we were in the air, I was shocked to feel as though we were just in a car. The hum of the plane was louder than I'd considered, but it was smooth. "Will it be bumpy again?" I asked, feeling a little queasy at the thought, despite the Dramamine.

"They'll tell us if they expect turbulence, but it'll be okay," he comforted me.

"I can't believe you did this," I told him, looking around at the plane again. I was on a freaking private jet. Chance was so down-to-earth and humble. We lived in a tiny two-bedroom house that we rented. It was easy for me to forget how he was raised, or the fact that his family were wealthy beyond my comprehension, except for moments like this, or anytime I visited his family's estate. It was surreal seeing how familiar this whole situation seemed to Chance at all.

"Amanda insisted," he reminded me.

"Like you argued," I challenged.

Chance chuckled in response. "I didn't," he admitted.

"I miss Toby," I blurted out.

Chance smiled softly, leaning in to kiss my temple. "He's probably being spoiled rotten as we speak, with all the walks, treats, and cuddles he can handle."

I swallowed, knowing he was right. I'd never had a pet before Toby. I knew I would love an animal if I ever got to have one, but I didn't realize how deeply that love would run until I met that little puppy in the shelter, that Chance had surprised me with only a couple months prior.

"Read your book, muse." He pointed to the e-reader in my hand. "It's a long flight."

But after an hour of Euripides, and having gotten more used to the plane, I found I was bored. Chance had been right, the flight itself was fine. I had nothing to worry about.

I turned to face Chance in my seat, watching him as he tapped on his tablet. But when his eyes darted up to meet mine, I noticed the anxious furrow to his brow had returned. I thought we'd gotten over the hard part of getting in the air, so I didn't understand why he was still acting so strangely.

"I can take this off, now that we're at altitude, right?" I motioned to the seatbelt around my waist.

Chance nodded, setting his tablet down.

I unclasped the buckle on mine, before doing the same to his, causing him to raise a brow. But when I crawled into his lap, my legs straddling his, his confusion morphed into his signature smirk. "And just what do you think you're doing, muse?"

"You seem stressed," I told him, snuggling into him, placing soft kisses against the column of his neck. "I thought you might want a distraction."

"A distraction?" He huffed. But he didn't fool me. I could hear the groan he withheld at the back of his throat and felt him harden beneath me. I also noticed he'd avoided my accusation.

I looked over to the closed door that separated us from the flight attendant's space and cockpit. "She won't come in here, will she?"

"Not unless we call her." He swallowed hard, his eyes going hazy as he regarded me.

"Then let's not call her." I smiled at him as I scooted back, standing just long enough to use my foot to tap his, indicating he needed to spread his legs for me.

"Violet..." he breathed, his tone reproachful, but his eyes simmering with desire.

I continued to grin up at him as I settled on my knees between his legs, running my palms up and down the top of his muscled thighs, over his pants. "Why are you so stressed, love?" I looked up at him through my lashes.

"I'm not—there's just—" He huffed another breath when my fingers made their way toward the bulge in his pants. He glanced over at the staff door again. "We shouldn't..."

"No, we shouldn't," I agreed with a Cheshire smile. Exhibitionism wasn't something that normally would have turned me on, but when else would I have the opportunity to join the mile high club with Chance?

"And you shouldn't keep avoiding the subject." I used my index and middle finger to walk up the line of his zipper toward the button of his pants, enjoying the way his chest was heaving as he watched me with rapt attention. "Why, Chance?"

Really I should have been above using sex to get what I wanted when it came to Chance, but he didn't keep secrets from me, so I felt like he'd done this to himself at the end of the day. And we liked to play with each other; I didn't think he'd mind.

"I just want you to have a good week," he confessed.

I sensed there was more to it, but I flicked open the button regardless. I raised a brow, waiting for more.

"I want it to be perfect," he continued, his voice raspy as he watched me.

I dragged the zipper down slowly. "Nothing is perfect, Chance," I replied softly, hoping he understood I meant that I didn't expect everything to be perfect, but also that it would be just because we were together.

"I'm worried if something goes wrong that you won't want to travel more." He finally got to the heart of it.

I cocked my head at his admission. "Something *will* go wrong," I told him, using the pad of my index finger to trail along the hem of his boxer briefs, delighting when I elicited a shiver from Chance. "But you'll be there, so it'll be okay. And I won't give up after one trip."

He swallowed hard, his gaze bouncing between my eyes and fingers.

"You can always talk to me about this stuff," I demurred as I pulled his cock free from its confines.

A breath wooshed out from him.

Warm, hard, but velvet in texture, I reveled in the weight of him in my hand, giving him a firm pump. "Chance," I called to him.

His eyes flicked to mine. "I will," he promised, his words a low rumble.

My lips quirked at his confirmation before I took the length of him in my mouth.

Chance hissed a breath at the feel of my tongue swirling around the tip. His head canted back against the hull of the plane behind him. "Fuck, baby..." he groaned as I sucked him harder. One of his hands came to mine, clutching at his thigh to keep me stable as I bobbed against his length. The other tangled into my hair, holding me against him with just the right amount of pressure that made my pussy pulse around nothing, but not so tight that I couldn't pull back if it was too much.

And that was how things always were with Chance. Not just when we were exploring each other, but in how we navigated our relationship. He always made sure it was never a question as to how much he wanted me, but he was so in tune with my emotions, expression, and moods that he knew precisely when to give me space or comfort.

The way Chance loved me was its own kind of addiction, and one I never wanted to be cured of.

His hand tightened in my hair as I took another strong pull of his cock with my mouth. I glanced up at him through my lashes to see him watching me through hooded eyes, his chest surging as he tried so very hard to keep his composure. But I knew from the way he continued to harden and grow in my mouth that he didn't have long left. The question was how he wanted this to end.

"Inside," he growled, answering my silent question.

I released him in a flash, shucking off my shoes and pants before straddling him again.

"You are a fucking goddess," he murmured as I positioned his cock at my entrance. We moaned in unison as I slowly slid down, sheathing him inside of me. "It'll never be enough..."

I smiled against him as I began to roll my hips, chasing the orgasm I could feel building low in my belly. Chance's arms were banded around me, one at the middle of my back, pressing me against him, and the other once again found purchase in my hair, this time at the base of my neck as he moved in tandem beneath me, no doubt pursuing his own release.

I cried out as his teeth scraped across the junction of my shoulder and neck before his lips latched there, pulling and sucking with the wet heat of his mouth. I knew it would leave a mark and secretly preened at the thought of him needing to do it at all.

I wanted him to mark me as his. I didn't care who saw it any longer. He was the only thing that mattered.

His hand left my neck and slipped between us. I released a strangled moan when his fingers found my clit. "Won't you come for me, muse?" he hummed against my neck.

Between his fingers and hips snapping against me, it didn't take long for me to unravel. The warmth built, stroke by stroke, and before I knew what was happening, I found myself spiraling into an abyss, my hips jerking against him as I climaxed.

Chance continued to pump into me, his lips finding mine in a feral and claiming kiss before he too succumbed to his need, his movements becoming erratic before he groaned through his release. Our hips slowed before they ceased entirely and I collapsed against Chance with him still buried inside me.

With his face burrowed against my neck, he whispered, "I can't wait to make you my wife."

3

Violet

Sitting in the back seat of another car, next to Chance, on the way to Amanda's new home, I finally felt as though I was actually on vacation. We'd left behind a snowy and frigid Maine, only to land in a temperate oasis, with green as far as the eye could see.

But back on solid ground, tucked in next to Chance, I found that I felt content. I had no papers to grade, no lessons to plan, no dog to take care of, although I never minded taking care of Toby. It was just us for the next week.

I watched the scenery roll past, my head resting against Chance's shoulder, his arm tightly wrapped around my waist. The landing of the small plane had been more abrupt than I'd thought it would be, but also faster, and I knew I'd be thinking about the fun we'd had on the plane for a long time.

The area of Northern California where Amanda and Hiram had chosen to settle down boasted all sorts of terrain, winding hills, forests, and eventually, even a sprawling coastal view as we finally reached their home.

Although I wouldn't have called it a home exactly...mansion or estate felt more appropriate.

After making it past a security gate and rural, but well-tended streets, with neat homes lining them, we finally turned off onto a narrow drive that wound through another copse of trees. The setting sun glimmered through the leaves, casting dappled shadows across Chance and me.

Peering past him, out the window, I couldn't help but give a small gasp when the forest gave way to a sprawling front lawn, at the end of which stood Cliffhaven, the name Amanda had dubbed her new home. And just beyond the house was a cliffside that abruptly cut through a view of the Pacific Ocean beyond, and the spectacular sunset which reflected off of the few clouds that lingered in the sky.

Cliffhaven lived up to its name. Amanda and her architect had somehow managed to blend traditional and modern design in the stately two-story residence. Large arched windows featured heavily, so much so that there were parts where you could see clear through the home and out to the waters beyond.

It was nothing short of spectacular.

And I said as much to Amanda, when she and Hiram greeted us the moment we exited the car.

"Welcome to Cliffhaven." Amanda pulled me in for a tight hug. I watched as Chance and Hiram shook hands behind her. "I have so many cute outfits for you!" she cheered.

Her thick blonde hair was pulled up into a ponytail, accentuating her modelesque bone structure, and perfect no-makeup look. She sported a chunky cream sweater and relaxed light-wash jeans. I'd never seen her dress so casually, but it suited her so well.

"Of course you do." I chuckled.

"How do you feel about athleisure?" She slung her arm around my shoulder and led me toward the front door, with the men following after us with the luggage.

"I'm stuck wearing slacks and button-ups for work, but I have like two pairs of leggings for the weekends," I told her.

My breath halted in my lungs when she pulled open the door, revealing the stunning open concept living and kitchen spaces. Directly to our right was a huge staircase leading up to the bedrooms, I presumed, but the sunset...

Through the glass windows, which it appeared could be folded open like origami, there was a completely unobstructed view of the ocean and setting sun. "Oh Amanda..."

"I know." She sighed, a smile evident in her voice. "You never get used to it. And I'm glad for it."

Other than the view, what really took my breath away was the cathedral ceilings with exposed wood beams. "Is that redwood?" I asked more rhetorically than anything.

"Reclaimed." Amanda's eyes lit up at the question.

The gable shape made the room somehow feel both cozy and cavernous at the same time, and just like the exterior, I was once again astounded by how she had managed to seamlessly blend modernity with such elegant timelessness.

She'd been smart to use a warmer-toned slightly off-white that made the room feel bright and airy without feeling stuffy or starch. Even the countertops were a warmer stone color, and the cabinetry was natural wood, which seemed to ground the kitchen space within the open floorplan.

Perhaps more than that, the house seemed so quintessentially Amanda, in every single detail, which I had no doubt she'd handpicked herself. I was proud of her.

"Drinks?" Hiram approached Amanda and me, holding out a champagne flute to each of us, then returning to the side table where he grabbed the remaining two, handing one off to Chance.

"I thought you might want something to help you relax after

a long day of travel." Amanda smiled at Chance and me. "And having you here is absolutely something to celebrate."

"To the next chapter." Chance smiled at me, clinking his glass against mine first, then his sister's, who smirked at the remark, and finally Hiram's, who repeated his sentiment.

Ever the stoic, Hiram was a man of few words, but standing in a dapper quarter-zip sweater and dark jeans, looking quite tall, dark, and handsome next to his wife, I couldn't help but think that they made such a beautiful pair.

"If you'll follow me, I must take you on a tour," Amanda practically squealed.

"Can't we get settled first?" Chance sighed. "The flight was over six hours and we've been traveling for more than eight."

"I want to see the house," I pleaded with Chance, using my free hand to take his. "Please. It'll be fast." While decompressing in the room for a little while sounded nice, the house was just so beautiful, and I wanted to see what I could before we lost all the daylight.

"Yes, it'll be fast." Amanda grinned.

"I've got some business to take care of, but I'll see you all at dinner." Hiram gracefully bowed out of the tour by giving Amanda a peck on the cheek before striding across the living room.

Amanda's warm gaze followed him briefly before she turned back to regard us. "Now, I do need to warn you, we'll have other guests at dinner."

"What guests?" Chance practically growled.

I squeezed his hand.

"We had some friends over the last few days, and they'll be leaving tomorrow," Amanda said casually. "Formal dining room on the left." She pointed toward an open doorway adjacent to the spacious kitchen island. "That's where dinner will be served at seven."

"You didn't mention any guests, Amanda." Chance was upset.

"Chance." Amanda stopped and turned around to glare at him. "It'll be fine," she said through her teeth.

My eyes ping-ponged between them, curious about the contextual tension of sibling rivalry I was missing in the exchange.

Chance pursed his lips, but remained quiet.

Satisfied the matter had been settled, Amanda continued. "We've got a private chef who will be arriving shortly and comes highly recommended." She turned toward me, a mischievous smile upon her lips. "Rumor has it, he's the go-to chef when A-listers visit the area."

I nodded in approval, although I was a heathen who ate mac and cheese out of a blue box if I was in a hurry, so fancy food was lovely, but perhaps wasted on my simple palate.

"I had to have a spa installed," Amanda told us as she walked us to a hallway behind the kitchen. "I can have a masseuse come out for you both later in the week if you'd like."

I glanced up at Chance. I'd never had a professional massage before.

"That'd be nice." He wrapped an arm around my waist, tugging me into his side.

"There's a sensory deprivation tank, sauna, and Himalayan salt meditation room," Amanda continued, waving at the open door to said spa, where I could see more windows letting in waning rays of the sunset.

"Gym's over here." She flicked her hand at another door farther down the hall. "Sorry, no pool, Chance. But plenty of weight and cardio machines, as well as a Pilates reformer and space for yoga, if that's your thing."

I held in a snort. I was not athletic in the least. It was more that I was terribly uncoordinated than anything else. Every time I'd stepped foot into a gym, I'd wound up breaking something, be it a machine, weight rack, or once a toe... because I'd tripped on a floor mat. Needless to say, I'd be steering clear of that space.

At the end of the hallway, before it dumped back out onto the far side of the kitchen, a final open door revealed a gorgeous room that had floor-to-ceiling windows along every single exposed wall. "And this is the sunroom." Amanda grinned, happily noting the awe in my expression.

"It's like the atrium at Harper House—just not round." I sighed happily.

Chance pulled me closer.

"I think so too." Amanda's gaze wandered across the space, filled with cozy lounge furniture, with a look of appreciation.

I noticed outside the sunroom, along the entirety of the backside of the house, was a large wood patio that stretched quite a ways, also dotted with lounge chairs and some bistro sets. Sitting in one of the chairs farther along the patio, was a blonde man paging through a magazine, his long legs crossed at the ankle, and glasses balancing precariously on his nose. How he managed to keep his attention on a magazine when the view was so spectacular was beyond me.

Amanda didn't seem to notice him as she led us back through the other side of the kitchen, across the length of the living room, and to an entrance on the far side. "Hiram's office is to the left." She motioned with one hand to a closed door. "And mine's at the front of the house." She motioned down the hall with the other. "But I just had to show you the library."

I perked up at that.

Chance chuckled at my side, clearly sensing my interest.

And sure enough, halfway down the hallway, Amanda opened the redwood double doors to reveal a capacious room lined with dark built-in shelving and a fireplace at the far side. The middle of the room held a balance of leather furniture and two large wood desks.

"You even have a rolling ladder." I couldn't contain my excitement.

"Think there's a hidden room behind any of the shelves?" Chance leaned down to whisper in jest, referencing the room we'd discovered at Harper House over the holidays, although it hadn't been behind a bookcase, like I'd suspected at the time.

"We might need to stay a few extra weeks to pull out all the books and check," I told him through a giggle.

"You're welcome to stay as long as you like," Amanda offered, having heard my comment. "But let's get you settled in upstairs before dinner, and I'm dying to show you the clothes I found for you." She squeezed my hand as she passed us to return to the hallway.

And once we made it toward the door she'd noted as her office, I realized we'd looped back around to the front of the house and the large staircase that led up to the second floor. Dutifully, Chance and I followed her up the steps as she proceeded to point out additional architectural details and specific design decisions she had made with the architect and why.

We stopped in front of a door just off the landing, and as Amanda reached out to open it, instead a young woman, maybe in her twenties, with dark curly hair that barely touched her shoulders, wearing all black, pulled open the door and stopped short when she saw the group of us.

Amanda's hand flew to her chest. "Ruth, you scared me." Amanda laughed, as if feeling silly for being frightened.

Ruth's cheeks reddened. "I'm sorry, Amanda," she said quietly.

"This is Ruth." Amanda stepped back to introduce the girl. "She's helping us keep the house running. Ruth, this is my brother, Chance, and his fiancée, Violet."

"It's nice to meet you." The girl gave both of us a soft handshake, only glancing up briefly through her fringe, but otherwise kept her gaze downward. "I brought up their luggage," she told Amanda.

"Oh, thank you." Amanda smiled at Ruth. "I forgot to ask Hiram."

"It's no problem," Ruth replied as she looked down at a

notification on her watch. “The chef’s arrived. I’ll make sure he gets set up.”

“Thank you, Ruth!” Amanda called after her. “Isn’t she a dear?” She beamed at both of us.

I couldn’t quite get a read on her, but dressed all in black, she was certainly a girl after my own heart.

“Now.” Amanda clapped her hands together, her attention suddenly focused on me. “I’ll give you twenty minutes, but then I must insist you come to my room and see all the beautiful things I’ve got to show you. We’re just at the end of the hall.” She motioned toward another set of double doors that I assumed led to the primary suite.

I opened my mouth to protest, but she interrupted me. “My house. My rules. I’ll see you in a moment.” She beamed before flitting toward her room and leaving Chance and me staring after her.

4

CHANCE

"Amanda, it's too much!" Violet stared at the clothing neatly laid out over the end of Amanda's bed. She'd curated a small selection of casual wear, athleisure, and a couple of cocktail dresses for my pint-sized fiancée. Violet was in distress, but I wanted to see her play dress-up, so I watched the two of them argue while lounging in a chair across the room.

"Please! Let me spoil you," Amanda argued. "I could have been a celebrity stylist in another life and this is the only way to live out that fantasy. Would you really deny me that?"

"I'm not a celebrity," Violet deadpanned, hands on hips as her gaze bounced back and forth between the clothes and her soon-to-be sister-in-law.

Amanda's jaw set in a firm line, likely calculating what offensive to try next. She turned to glance at me. "Is she always this stubborn?"

"Always." I chuckled in agreement.

Violet spun around to shoot me a death glare that made me half-hard thinking about how she'd channel that wrath into our lovemaking later. I loved it when she was feisty.

Observing the two of them sparring was always amusing, but more than that, it made my heart swell, thinking about how far Violet had come in such a short time. The fact that she got along with my family, let alone seemed to have actually become close with Amanda, despite the geographical distance, was a feat in itself.

All Violet ever wanted was somewhere to belong. She'd belonged to me from the moment I'd laid eyes on her, but it hadn't occurred to me as we'd fallen in love that I'd be able to help her belong to other people and places as well, surrounding her with the love and community she'd been lacking her entire life.

Violet's eyes pleaded with me over Amanda's shoulder. And when she mouthed, "help me," I held back a laugh, knowing it would get me in more trouble than it was worth.

"What about a compromise?" I suggested.

Both women turned to regard me. Violet's shoulders slumped in relief, and Amanda's eyes narrowed with suspicion.

"Violet, why don't you pick a couple of outfits—"

Amanda huffed as she planted her hands on her hips.

"Amanda, we don't have room at our house for everything anyway. That way, Violet gets a few new things that are her choice, and you get to play stylist." I raised a brow, waiting for a response.

"You have to pick at least one of each category," Amanda demanded.

"Okay." Violet swallowed, her eyes finding mine with a silent thanks.

"But I want to see you try on all the dresses." I smirked when Violet's glare hit me once again.

Amanda suppressed a giggle at the thought. She leaned over the bed and plucked a dress from the pile. "Start with this one." She thrust it at Violet. "Off you go." She all but shoved her into the bathroom before Violet had a chance to challenge her.

Amanda approached me, sinking into the chair next to me while we waited for Violet to emerge.

"The dress is sorted," she said under her breath. "It's hidden away in Hiram's office for safekeeping."

I shot a look at the closed bathroom door.

"It's going to make you cry when you see her in it." Amanda appeared amused at the thought.

"I think I'll cry no matter what she's wearing," I whispered, already feeling the emotion well inside of me at the thought of marrying her.

"Stop, or you'll make me swoon." She batted my arm playfully.

"You're sure she won't be upset I'm surprising her with the elopement?" I swallowed hard, needing the reassurance that I was doing the right thing.

"It will be everything she said she wanted. Small. Intimate. Simple." Amanda repeated the words I'd continuously expressed to her regarding the whole affair.

I'd woken up in the middle of the night almost a month ago in a panic about losing Violet, probably a nightmare. But looking at her sleeping soundly next to me, my heart ached for her, and even though it hadn't been long since I'd proposed, I found I simply couldn't wait another moment to be married to her. I longed to be connected to her eternally.

The impulse was unreasonable and sharp, but every time I looked at her, I felt the need, deep and low in my gut. I think

Violet viewed things differently than me because she'd told me she'd never thought she'd get married before meeting me. Marriage meant something different to her. Not that it wasn't serious, but only that she would have been content to just be partners without anything official, for the rest of our days.

And that should have been good enough for me. I wasn't worried about her going anywhere, but I just needed to know that the whole world recognized our union to the depth at which we did. So I'd done the only thing I could think of...I'd called my sister.

Within hours, I had a string of multiple emails with ideas and spreadsheets and mood boards. Amanda was in her element and understood what Violet would appreciate better than most. Because even though my sister lavished Violet with gifts, much to her chagrin, Violet and I both knew each piece had been hand-selected and curated precisely for Violet's tastes alone. Amanda showed her love through thoughtful gestures and by noticing the things that other people didn't, which was likely why most of the clothing was black, Violet's favorite color. Amanda was an expert at seeing people, and making sure they felt seen.

Despite their squabble over the clothes moments ago, I knew Violet always felt so loved, and so beautiful wearing the clothes Amanda picked out for her, even if she had a hard time accepting gifts or showing her appreciation without refusing things multiple times first.

"I worry she'll feel pressured or disappointed if it's not what she was envisioning," I voiced my worries aloud.

"Hasn't she offered to do a courthouse wedding with you multiple times already?" Amanda chided. "And if she's willing to do a courthouse wedding, what I have planned is a million times better. So I have no doubt it will exceed any limited expectations she may have. Although it sounds like the only thing she wants is for you to be waiting for her at the end of the aisle."

I gave a deep exhale. I knew Amanda was right. And, truly, I wasn't afraid Violet would change her mind...I was only afraid I was going to get it wrong. I only had one shot at this. It had to be perfect, for my perfect, beautiful, brilliant little muse.

"I need help with the zipper," Violet called out as she opened the door to the bathroom.

I felt my jaw tick as I assessed her in a tight-fitting black lace cocktail dress with a bustier-style top and a bottom that looked more like a pencil skirt...my favorite type of skirt on Violet. My mouth went dry as I allowed my eyes to peruse her figure in the garment. She was a fucking vision. And she was mine.

"You're wearing that to dinner," I asserted.

"Don't tell me what to do," Violet sassed, a gleam of mirth in her expression.

"No, but seriously, you look bangin' in that dress, and you definitely should wear it to dinner." Amanda smiled, pleased with herself as she made her way to Violet to help her fasten the dress. I made sure to pay attention so I knew how to take it off her in a hurry later.

Violet took a deep breath, but it seemed she wasn't preparing to put up a fight.

Good, I thought, *we can fight for fun later.*

"Follow me, I've got shoe options in my closet and I think a headband would be the right touch to finish off the look." Amanda looped her arm through Violet's, tugging her toward the walk-in closet. "You too, big brother. We need your approval."

"I don't need his approval," Violet disagreed.

Oh yes, you do.

Amanda's closet was half the size of our small house in Maine, filled with a colorful array of clothing and textures, racks of dresses, and drawers I was sure were filled to the brim with everything else. One wall was entirely made of neat rows of shoes and heels in all shapes, colors, and sizes.

"Do you think you have enough?" I joked, leaning against the doorframe.

“One can never have enough clothing.” Amanda stuck her tongue out at me.

“I don’t know about that...” Violet trailed off when Amanda’s eyes narrowed on her.

“I think the suede d’orsay pointed toe or maybe the open-toed option with the slim ankle strap would go best.” Amanda pulled one of each style from shoeboxes she had set on a bench near the island in the middle of the closet.

“They’re like six inches!” Violet whined. “I’ll break my neck.”

“They’re only four, and you’ll be sitting all dinner.” Amanda was poised and ready with her rebuttal.

“But I’ll have to walk up and down the stairs.”

“And that’s why you have a sturdy fiancé to help you keep your balance.” Amanda gestured to me, still at the threshold.

Violet grimaced, but grabbed the suede option.

“As for the headband...” Amanda crossed the closet and moved to a cabinet door that was hiding a safe. She punched in a code and then pressed her thumb to a screen before the door opened, revealing a large display of what I assumed was heirloom jewelry from Grandma Mitzi, neatly arranged on black velvet stands and displays to showcase every piece. There was even a light that went on when the door had opened, to adequately illuminate the items inside, making the whole setup look like a boutique jewelry store display.

"I think pearls would be a nice touch." Amanda plucked a silver headband from a row of others, with delicate ornate metal detailing, small pearls, and glittering diamonds woven throughout the design.

"Amanda..." Violet's tone was hushed in its admonishment. She once again was walking a fine line between wanting to wear the piece and thinking that she wasn't worthy of its splendor.

Amanda approached Violet, tucking her hair behind her ears, then gently placed the headband on her, making some minor adjustments. She stepped back, admiring her work. "Yes, that feels right."

With a flourish, Amanda stepped aside so Violet could see herself in the full-length mirror next to the jewelry cabinet. I strode across the room and came up behind Violet. A sigh escaped her lips as she felt the warmth of my hand at her waist.

"Aren't you stunning," I whispered against her ear.

Amanda smirked behind us, clearly pleased with my acceptance and encouragement.

"You just like me in skirts and dresses." Violet gave me a knowing look in the mirror.

"I also like it when you wear things that allow you to shine as brightly as I always see you," I commented, giving her hip a squeeze.

Her eyes went soft at the compliment.

There was a quiet knock at the door that interrupted the spell cast on the three of us. We all turned to regard Ruth at the entrance to the closet. "The chef said dinner will be ready in thirty minutes. He asked me to tell you he'd love to keep things on schedule so he can serve the food at the optimal timing and temperature," she delivered the message.

"Right." Amanda nodded. "Thank you, Ruth."

Ruth flashed a quick smile then took her leave.

"Violet, why don't you go decide what pieces you'd like to take with you. I need to show Chance his clothing for dinner," Amanda stated.

"My clothing?" I guffawed.

"Not so fun when you're the paper doll, is it?" Violet laughed as she slipped out of my hold to return to the bedroom.

Amanda rolled her eyes. "You're welcome!" she called after Violet. Turning her attention toward me, she said, "It's just a black dress shirt and slacks. Relax." She paused, craning her neck to peek out of the doorway to Violet standing across the room examining the outfits on the bed. "I thought you might want me to hang on to the rings, just in case," she said, her voice low.

I nodded, pulling a slim box out of my pants pocket, feeling the weight of the rings as I passed them to my sister. "Can I see?" she asked.

I nodded, pleased as a smile curled her lips in admiration when she saw the set together, along with the simple band I'd chosen for myself. "Perfect," Amanda breathed, her glassy eyes glancing up at me briefly before she turned to neatly tuck the box inside the safe, then closed it.

Violet had needed to get her engagement ring, a family heirloom I'd gotten from my mother over Christmas, resized, as it was slightly too large for her fingers. However, she'd been loath to part with it. So I'd conspired with Amanda to get a replica made and swapped out the rings when she was sleeping. The resizing also gave me the opportunity to work with a local jeweler to create a custom wedding band that would perfectly fit around the unique setting of the vintage ring and match the art deco style precisely, as well as designing one for myself that harmonized.

"She's in good hands." Amanda regarded me as she handed me a garment bag. "You don't have anything to worry about."

"Thank you."

5

VIOLET

"We could just stay up here." Chance looked up at me through his lashes as he knelt before me, helping to put my heels on. Well, that's what he said he was doing, but in reality, he was just running his hand up and down my calf, giving me goosebumps, trying to convince me to forgo dinner and break in the bed with him.

"Your sister has gone through a lot of trouble for us." I removed his hand from my leg and stood from the end of the bed, watching Chance as he rose in tandem. "It's the least we can do." I stepped toward him to straighten his collar.

Amanda had dressed her brother all in black, and I had a sneaking suspicion she'd done it for me. He looked so incredibly handsome in his slim-fitting black shirt and slacks, complete with shiny black loafers that I had a feeling had cost a small fortune, based on the red soles.

"You look like a dark and brooding mob boss." I bit my lip, looking up at Chance, running my palms down his chest.

"Oh yeah?" He quirked a brow, leaning forward to run the tip of his nose along my temple as his hands squeezed my hips. "Maybe we should skip dinner to play mafioso and captive," he whispered darkly.

I felt my cheeks heat imagining how thoroughly he'd ravish me. But I was determined to make it down to dinner. It was only polite.

Fighting my instincts, I pushed against him, but it only made Chance pull me closer, his hands traveling farther down, skimming my hips, then cupping my backside in his large palms.

"Are you not wearing underwear?" He reared back, confusion and arousal etched on his face.

I threw him a smirk before taking the short window of opportunity to pivot around him and sprint across the room to the door. Well, sprint was a generous word—I was wearing heels after all. But I surprised Chance enough to make it just out of his reach.

"Get back here, muse," he whisper-shouted after me, as I'd

flung open the door to scramble out into the hallway. "I'm not done with you."

But only a short way down the hall, I stopped, hearing a heated argument occurring on the other side of a closed door to the room next to ours. Having been hot on my heels, Chance slammed into my back, his arms going around my waist to steady us both from the impact. "You're not very good at letting me chase you; we'll have to practice more." Chance chuckled, nuzzling his face against the crook of my neck.

I turned slightly to make eye contact with him and brought my finger up to my mouth, signaling him to be silent.

His brow furrowed, but then he heard the voices and his expression shifted into understanding.

We couldn't hear whatever the couple was arguing about, it was only clear that it was a man and a woman, and whatever was going on was quite contentious.

"I've had enough," the male voice shouted loudly. "I'm going to be late."

Chance and I shared a wide-eyed look and decided to take that as our cue to get the hell out of there, rushing toward the front staircase before we were discovered eavesdropping. His grip remained firm as I slowly descended the stairs, careful not to trip in the heels.

"What we started upstairs isn't over," Chance growled when we finally made it to the first floor, releasing his hold on me, only to slip his fingers between mine.

I looked up at him coquettishly and blinked. "I don't know what you're talking about."

His lips were upturned in amusement.

We did so love our games.

"Finally! We've been waiting down here for ages," Amanda shouted as we entered the formal dining room, just off the entryway. Her legs were propped in Hiram's lap and it appeared he was giving her a foot massage. "Where is everyone?"

I shrugged, not wanting to tattle on the couple upstairs.

Amanda swung her legs off Hiram's thighs and gripped the table to balance herself as she slipped her shoes back on. "Thank you, baby." She leaned forward, pressing a chaste kiss to his lips.

Hiram's cheeks went slightly pink at the action, which I found positively adorable.

"We're on time." Chance glanced down at his watch, then held it out toward Amanda, as if she would be able to read it across the table.

She rolled her eyes at his antics.

"Where would you like us to sit?" I asked Amanda politely, knowing she likely had a seating arrangement in mind, although there weren't place cards out on the large dining table, which was elegantly outfitted with short burgundy floral table arrangements, and matching chargers at each seat, of which there were seven in total, leaving the far end of the table empty.

Appropriately, Amanda was positioned at the head of the table, with Hiram on her right. "Violet, I want you next to me." She pointed to the chair on her left, "And I suppose my brother can sit next to you," she added, her tone teasing as she shrugged at Chance, as though he was an afterthought. I knew better, and I enjoyed their version of sibling antagonism. Pointed, but never mean.

"Very kind of you, sister dear," he replied through his teeth as he pulled out my chair for me.

"Thank you." I smiled up at him.

"You want a drink, sweetheart?" he asked, glancing in the corner to a low credenza that was adorned with a tray of spotless wineglasses and champagne flutes, as well as an assortment of wine and a bottle of champagne chilling in an ice bucket.

"The champagne was nice," I replied.

He nodded, making his way to the drinks. "Want anything?"

He glanced over at Amanda and Hiram, who both shook their heads, half-full glasses already in front of them.

"Who else are we dining with tonight?" I crossed my legs, resting my elbows on the table to lean toward Amanda conspiratorially, although I knew it wasn't proper etiquette.

Amanda's lips quirked, just like Chance's would, as if she was thrilled to have a secret to share. "Well, I can't wait for you to meet Marcus, my architect. He's such a character!" She beamed. "Widower to an old-money heiress who was quite his senior, he's a notorious rake and a shameless flirt, but has the most amazing stories."

I could only laugh at her description.

"Have you been reading too many bodice rippers? Who uses the term 'rake' these days?" Chance quipped as he set down two glasses of champagne on the table before taking his seat next to me, making sure to slide his as close to mine as possible.

"You're just jealous my vocabulary is more advanced than yours."

"I'm an English teacher, Amanda. I'm quite certain my vocabulary is more robust."

Hiram and I exchanged a knowing look across the table, shaking our heads at our partners' antics.

"If he's a widower to an heiress, why is he still working as an architect?" I turned my attention back to Amanda, disrupting the sibling tête-à-tête.

"Well, architecture is his passion, and while they were married, she gave him access to the most elite circle of clientele, which of course was how I found him. Now he gets his pick of whatever projects he wants to work on," Amanda offered, implying that her home design had been unique enough for him to deign to work on. "You'll love him."

I nodded, skeptical about her assessment.

"Then there's Gray, one of Hiram's colleagues," Amanda continued.

"I wouldn't call him a colleague." Hiram snorted.

Amanda chuckled. I sensed a story.

"His name is Gray?" Chance quipped.

"Well Grayson—Grayson Bennett," she provided his full name. "But he goes by Gray. He's some tech genius trying to get Hiram to invest in his latest venture."

Hiram exhaled a heavy sigh beside her. Again, I sensed there was so much more to this that I was missing.

"It started as a lunch meeting and somehow turned into them staying over the weekend." Amanda patted Hiram's hand on the table.

"Them?" I cocked my head.

"Oh yes, he brought his wife with him—or maybe she invited herself along. Probably the latter. I think she wants to be my best friend." Amanda shrugged, before taking a sip of her drink, as if people wanting to become her best friend was an everyday occurrence for her.

Amanda must have seen the quizzical look on my face, so she provided more context. "You might have heard of her: Zara Sable?"

Chance and I shook our heads in unison.

"Oh, well, she's some sort of social media famous wellness guru and former reality persona, shilling all sorts of supplements and unsanctioned medical advice." Amanda half laughed, her annoyance with the woman evident in her description. "She's been trying to peer pressure me into attending her next celebrity wellness retreat all weekend, but I'm just not into all that woo woo cult shit, ya know?"

I didn't, but I nodded anyway.

And suddenly, as if summoned, the woman I suspected was Zara Sable wafted into the dining room wearing a silk outfit in various tones of ivory and taupe, along with matching sandals. Her pants were so wide, I almost mistook them for a skirt upon first glance, with an elegant chemise tucked into the high waist. But the real showstopper was her billowing floor-length duster, with kimono sleeves. There was enough material, it had me craning my neck to try and figure out if it actually had a train. I couldn't see well enough to make a decision either way.

The neutral colors only managed to accentuate her deep auburn hair, set in perfectly coiffed, beachy waves that fell past her shoulders. Equally as impeccable was her matching soft-white mani-pedi and no-makeup makeup look. Both of which I was sure had taken hours to perfect, but she seemed like the kind of woman who would claim to have woken up looking that good, thanks to her nightly curcumin tincture, which you too can buy, using discount code ZARA on her website for ten percent off your first order.

It didn't surprise me that while Amanda had told me the dinner was cocktail attire, Zara had shown up in her own version, walking in as the main character of her own narrative, impervious to those around her. And I had to admit, I could kind of see the cult-leader appeal. She was stunning and had an aura about her that I could imagine would be easy to fall prey to if you didn't know better.

"Amanda, darling, you look divine!" Her voice was soft and melodic. She sauntered over to Amanda, who stood to greet her as they exchanged air kisses.

It took everything in me not to roll my eyes, although I knew from having attended many events at Chance's parents' estate that this was the proper etiquette for women of their stature.

I didn't understand why a polite handshake or hug wouldn't do the trick.

"Hiram, always a pleasure." She stuck out her hand awkwardly, with her fingers pointing down. I wondered if she expected him to kiss the top of her hand? But instead he only shook her fingers woodenly, sporting a grimace masquerading as a forced smile.

"Zara, this is my brother, Chance, and his fiancée, Violet." Amanda gestured to Chance and me.

Her head turned to regard us as we stood to greet her, as if she hadn't realized we were in the room until that moment, because I imagined unless a formal introduction was made, she would have assumed we were lesser beings unworthy of her time or eye contact.

"My, aren't you handsome." She approached Chance, extending her limp hand to him, just as she'd offered it to Hiram.

I could feel him bristle next to me as he reached out to shake her fingers, just as Hiram had done. I did not miss the fact that Hiram was trying desperately to hold back his laughter behind Zara.

"You look like you work out." Zara reached out, sliding her palm down his chest before Chance took a step back, glaring at her for the unwanted touch. I felt my jaw clench and hackles rise as I regarded her, while she still refused to acknowledge me.

"I'd love to get your routine for my followers." She completely ignored his discomfort as she smiled up at him.

Perhaps sensing my impending rage, Chance slipped an arm around my waist and leaned in conspiratorially to Zara to say, "Just chasing this one around keeps me plenty fit," as he tugged me closer to his side.

I glowered up at him. While I was pleased to hear him reassert our relationship status, the double meaning in his words was not lost on me.

Zara's eyes bounced to mine, and for a brief moment, as her assessing gaze swept over me, I felt as though she was asking herself what on earth a man like Chance was doing slumming it with a plebeian like me. "Aren't you a cute little thing?" she dissented, reaching out a finger to boop my fucking nose.

My eyes widened, but before I could open my mouth to snarl at her, Amanda intervened. "Let's get you a drink, Zara!" Her sing-song voice was a little too loud. Amanda glanced at me quickly, an apology buried in her expression along with a plea not to escalate the situation.

"I'll poison her drink with laxatives if you want," Chance whispered.

I clamped a hand over my mouth to stop a giggle from erupting at the thought.

"Oh, yes." Zara had missed our exchange entirely. "Where's your girl? The one with the blue aura?" Zara peered around the room.

Unfortunately for Ruth, she made the mistake of entering at the most inopportune time. "There you are." Zara waved her hand at Ruth, whose own hands were full of a large tray of appetizers she clearly wanted to set down. "I'd like a white Negroni, but with Lillet Blanc instead of vermouth, and no citrus expression, just the peel resting."

Ruth's face betrayed her, looking nothing if not bewildered. "We just have wine and champagne." She glanced over Zara's shoulder to the credenza where the bottles and glasses had been set out for the dinner guests.

Zara's light smile faltered. "I suppose I'll have an orange wine then. Preferably low-intervention."

"I don't think we have that either." Ruth turned to Amanda, who had joined Hiram in holding back their laughter at the entire exchange. I watched as Ruth's shoulders relaxed slightly when she realized she wasn't the only one in the room to think Zara's request and demeanor ridiculous.

"Hiram, help Ruth," Amanda instructed, rounding the table to make it over to Zara. "Let's see what we can find over here." She redirected the woman to the available drinks.

"We're not big on cocktails. I hope you'll forgive me for not having a fully stocked bar. We haven't been here long, so I'm not as practiced at hosting in the space."

"I can give you referrals for excellent event planning services so you can hire a bartender for your next soiree."

"That would be wonderful," Amanda agreed.

"It's so hard to find good help these days, you know," Zara added.

I felt my jaw go tight again at her words, but Chance's hand squeezed my backside, momentarily distracting me from my ire.

"Oh good, we're doing drinks? I'll take a triple whiskey. Whatever's the oldest vintage you have on hand."

I knew immediately the newest addition was Grayson Bennett. He walked in with a swagger like he owned the place, exactly how I imagined an aging Silicon Valley tech bro would operate. Also ignoring Amanda's requested dress code, he was wearing light-wash jeans and immaculate white sneakers, but had dressed them up with a half-unbuttoned white oxford, topped with a navy sports coat. He wore his salt-and-pepper hair cropped and the coloring continued into his short, well-groomed beard. Everything about Gray oozed new money know-it-all.

"Hey, baby." He approached Zara from behind, nuzzling into her neck before she abruptly pulled away from him with a tight smile.

They were definitely the couple we'd heard arguing from the hallway. I cut a glance at Chance with a raised eyebrow at the interaction and he smirked, as if he'd come to the same conclusion himself.

"Amanda's getting me a drink." She shot him a pointed glare before ignoring him and returning her attention to Chance's sister, who was pouring her a glass of each bottle that was out on the table to taste, as Zara couldn't make up her mind.

"Hiram!" Gray called out as he turned around. "Where are you hiding the good shit? I finished off what you had left in the office."

Hiram blew out a frustrated breath as he helped Ruth finish placing the last of what appeared to be the first course out on the table. Gray was oblivious.

"Ruth, please get Gray a glass of Macallan when you have a chance," Amanda instructed her from across the room. "And if you could please ask the chef if a Chablis will pair well with dinner for Zara. If he says, yes, please grab a bottle from the wine fridge in the kitchen."

"I take it neat." Gray flicked a hand at Ruth before she could leave the room, as he dropped into the chair next to Chance.

"Oh, I have you on the opposite side of the table, Gray." Amanda frowned.

Unsurprisingly Gray ignored her. I caught myself mid-eye roll, thinking of my entitled students who often had selective hearing when it came to instruction.

"So what do you do?" Gray planted his elbows on the table, leaning forward toward Chance. I wondered if Gray had a sixth sense for money. It seemed like he could smell it on Chance. Maybe it was just the red-soled loafers that had tipped him off.

It was going to be a long night.

6

CHANCE

"The party has arrived!" The final guest at Amanda's dinner party, which had already gone awry, in my opinion, threw his hands out as he entered the dining room next to Ruth, almost knocking the drinks from her grip in the process.

"Marcus, darling! Where have you been all day!" Zara exclaimed, abandoning Amanda, who frankly looked relieved, and made her way to Marcus, taking the glass of white wine he extended to her.

I could quickly see how the architect had managed to woo an elderly heiress. Floppy blonde hair and blue eyes, hidden behind tortoiseshell glasses gave him a look of boyish charm, and the moment he spoke, he simply oozed charisma. His look, paired with the black turtleneck and dark suit, gave him a look that hinted at his profession but still invited intrigue into his persona.

"And for you, Grayson." Marcus set the glass of expensive scotch in front of Gray. I found it curious that he knew the couple well enough to know which drink belonged to whom. Perhaps Ruth had told him, and I supposed the choices were stereotypical if one considered gender.

Marcus dipped to whisper something to Ruth before she retreated, the words causing her to blush as she darted back to the kitchen.

"Don't worry, we'll have plenty of time to talk about your house back in the city." He greeted Zara with air kisses as she sidled up next to him, running her fingers down his arm.

Upon taking a sip of the wine, she made a sour face before slipping back into the mask of perfected indifference. It seemed anything other than her initial drink order wouldn't do. She set the full glass down on the table.

The moment Zara moved out of his line of sight, his gaze snagged on Violet, who was slumped in her chair next to me doing a poor job of hiding a scowl, arms crossed over her chest like a petulant child, unable to hide her annoyance with our new dinner companions.

God, I fucking love her.

"*Who* is this stunning creature!?" Marcus exclaimed as he approached her. My hand tightened around her thigh under the table reflexively causing Violet's eyes to snap to mine in question before swinging to Marcus.

"Where has Amanda been hiding you?" He lit up, reaching forward to grab her hand without her having offered it, only to place a kiss on the top of it, which had my blood boiling.

"New England." Violet frowned. "You must be the architect." She glanced over to me and cocked her head when she saw the look on my face. Was my unfounded jealousy so obvious? Her lips twitched, eyes still locked on mine.

The game was on, and she was a little too excited to play. I'd make her pay for it later.

"It's such a pleasure to meet the mastermind behind this unparalleled design." Violet gestured to the home around us, her personality shifting on a dime as she adopted a new character to entertain her admirer.

"Amanda has such a well-cultivated eye and discerning taste that pairs so well with my own aesthetic preferences." He beamed at her, wedging himself between her and me to lean against the dining table, forcing me to sever the connection with Violet.

Her eyes cut to mine again, as if to silently acknowledge that she felt the loss.

"It's simply a marvel, with the marriage you've made between traditional and coastal, with elements of sustainability throughout the space," she noted, looking up at him through her lashes and biting her bottom lip.

Anyone else would think her attention was squarely on Marcus, but I knew better. Those microexpressions were meant solely for me. Her flirting with him was meant to push me. We both knew she held no interest in him. She only had eyes for me, and I'd make sure she remembered that the next time we were alone.

"So what brings you out to California?" Marcus changed topics.

"My fiancé, Amanda's brother." She motioned to me, her eyes finally returning to mine, allowing the blood in my veins to cool to a low simmer.

Marcus stood, stepping back from the table so he could get a good look at me. His face fell as he assessed me. "Chance Harper." I stuck out my hand, making sure to grip his with extra firmness. Childish perhaps, but it sent a message nonetheless.

"Nice to meet you." He gave me a tight smile. "When's the wedding?"

"Oh, we don't have a date yet." Violet shrugged. Her nonchalance was intentional. I smiled inwardly, knowing she was wrong. She'd be my wife in less than three days if all went to plan.

"I see," Marcus replied, and a coy glint in his eyes unsettled me, as if to say her being unmarried was as good as single.

What he didn't know was that Violet Price was a viper, and she'd eat a man like him for breakfast, if given the opportunity. Now wouldn't that be fun to witness?

Marcus's attention snagged on Ruth as she slipped into the room and placed what looked like a mug of tea in front of Amanda before whispering something to her, and then leaving the room again just as quickly as she'd come. Marcus's eyes never left her form. Perhaps Amanda's notion of his rakish behavior wasn't so exaggerated after all. It seemed that every woman in the room was fodder for his charms.

"Please take your seats and enjoy the first course!" Amanda announced loudly, interrupting the discussion at and around the table. "The chef is on a tight schedule with the weather coming in overnight."

Unfortunately, dinner was about as enjoyable as I'd expected, and I regretted not pressuring Violet more to skip the affair entirely. But nothing could be done, as Amanda would have had my head if I'd decided to excuse myself for the bathroom and failed to return.

Gray mansplained his tech startup, Atmosync, "a wearable that tracked mood and emotional state via biometrics to provide environmental optimizations through integrations with existing smart home systems," but it sounded a bit too far-fetched for my liking, so I instead focused on slowly moving my hand farther and farther up Violet's thigh, seeing how far I could get up her dress before she'd start squirming or forcefully remove me, only for me to start my slow ascent again.

She hadn't worn panties on purpose. She'd done it to herself. She knew how crazy that drove me. I didn't stand a chance. I'd been hard as a fucking rock since the moment she'd come out of the bathroom wearing that flimsy lace dress. If she wanted me to suffer, she was winning, but that didn't mean I wasn't going to fight back...or play fair.

"You should consider investing," Gray hinted with a piss-poor attempt at subtlety.

What Gray didn't know was that while Amanda had explained every minute design decision during the house tour, Hiram had enlightened me about the company Gray was trying to raise funds for, and how put off he was that he couldn't seem to get rid of the pair of leeches since the moment they'd crossed paths.

Gray was clearly in over his head, as the other co-founder of Atmosync had recently left without fighting for any stake in the company. And Gray himself had a shady entrepreneurial past full of MLMs, grossly overvalued companies, and a trail of investors that had lost gobs of money. Failed investments were par for the course in the venture capitalism game, especially in Silicon Valley, but after a long string of them, it left a permanent miasma of radioactivity lingering around Gray. His desperation made that quite evident.

"Oh didn't he tell you?" Violet interrupted our conversation, a note of mischief in her tone. "He was disinherited years ago. Quite the scandal. Our meager teachers' salaries don't leave much room for investments after we've had to pay for rent and groceries."

Gray's face went red. I wasn't sure if it was from embarrassment or anger that he'd wasted the last half hour pitching a working class mark. Most likely the latter, I decided after a moment, seeing the vein in his neck pulse.

I pursed my lips, holding back laughter. While I preferred to work so I didn't have to dip into my trust fund or rely on my parents in any way, the large sum remained intact and accessible. Which Violet full well knew, as we had recently been in a stalemate over the small but cozy home that we rented, which the owner had informed me he would be happy to sell to us.

However, Violet wanted to contribute, but wasn't in a financial spot to be able to do so. I'd also offered to pay off her student loans and mother's house, but she'd refused me on multiple occasions and gotten mad enough I knew not to bring it up. I understood how much it meant to her to take care of herself, but sometimes I wanted to take care of her too.

More than once, I'd wondered if I should just pay everything off in secret and risk that her ire might subside after the shock had worn off. But we were a team...partners...and although I disagreed with her, worried her pride was getting in the way of practicality, respecting her boundaries was much more important in the long run.

I was building a forever with Violet, and I'd be damned if I was going to risk putting that in jeopardy.

"You're welcome," Violet murmured under her breath.

I slipped my hand farther up her thigh, giving her a squeeze as I leaned in to say, "Thank you, muse."

Laughter erupted across the table as Marcus regaled Zara with another story about some celebrity that she insisted she was best friends with...except she'd claimed no less than four other famous best friends throughout the dinner. It seemed they were well paired with their penchant for name-dropping.

I didn't miss the small touches and glances that lasted a moment too long. If I didn't know that Zara was married to Gray, whom she was happy to ignore, I might think that Marcus was her partner.

"How long have the two of you known each other?" Violet asked Marcus, her eyes darting between him and Zara, perhaps noting the same body language I had.

"We've only just met this weekend!" Zara exclaimed. "Can you believe it? But Gray and I have been looking for an architect of our own to develop a private compound up in wine country, and it's simply kismet that Marcus was here this weekend, and perfect for the job."

Marcus gave Zara a coy grin before turning his attention back to Violet. "How long have the two of you been together?" He motioned between us.

"About a year and a half," Violet rounded up. Although I suppose we'd met eighteen months prior, and she'd always been mine from the moment I saw her. "We got engaged over Christmas," she added.

"But no date yet." Marcus pursed his lips, recalling Violet's earlier admission.

I sensed her bristle next to me, feeling the accusation in his words. As if us not having a date somehow discounted our relationship, of which he knew nothing.

"It won't be too much longer," I assured Marcus, still wary of his interest in my fiancée.

Violet's face tilted to look at me, a soft smile on her lips before turning to regard Marcus. "Sorry to disappoint you."

He chuckled, as if he found her words a challenge.

"You think he could make you come with his tongue as quickly as I do?" I whispered soft and low just next to her ear.

Violet's face went crimson as she visibly gulped. "I'm going to kill you," she ground out quietly enough that only I could hear her.

"Maybe next time you'll think twice before going to dinner without panties, just to tease me." I smiled as I nuzzled against her hair.

A sharp yelp pulled Violet and I from our little bubble.

"Dammit, Gray!" Zara snapped as she stood from the table, narrowly missing getting his spilled drink on her flowing outfit.

"I'm sorry about the Macallan." Gray frowned at Hiram, who looked like he was at his wit's end and doing his very best not to blow up.

"It's okay, Gray. Accidents happen." Amanda gave him a tight smile, flagging down Ruth as she entered the dining room with what appeared to be a fresh cup of tea in one hand.

Amanda had been unusually quiet over dinner. Although I supposed she'd been stuck with these nightmare guests against her will for a couple days. Who could blame her? I didn't envy the position she and Hiram were in. Most people would assume to just usher them out as politely as possible, but in certain levels of society, even the most benign actions could be easily misinterpreted and cause unintentional consequences.

Amanda, like my mother before her, was a master of etiquette and propriety. Although Zara and Gray at the very least seemed to have outstayed their already tenuous welcome, Amanda was smart enough to know that kicking them out could damage countless society relationships. And while she was establishing herself in a new area, that could be disastrous for my sister and brother-in-law, who were looking to set down roots.

Ruth set the tea down in front of Amanda and listened intently as my sister gave her instructions. Hiram seemed to relax a fraction, with help on the way. Both he and my sister seemed so comfortable and trusting around Ruth. I wondered if they'd known her before moving, as they'd only settled in California shortly after the holidays a few months prior.

Ruth herself came across as a hard worker, and reserved her warmth for Amanda and Hiram alone, keeping a neutral, almost detached, expression when interacting with anyone else. After cleaning Gray's mess, she refilled his drink and then tucked herself into the corner of the room, waiting... assessing...observing.

More than once I caught her gaze lingering on Violet, with whom she seemed particularly fascinated.

She could join the club.

I wondered if it was the striking duality that Violet always projected. Confident and poised in one breath and imploding in on herself with the next, although I'd notably seen so much more of the former in the past six months as her therapy sessions really started to pay off.

Violet was such a contrast to the other three dinner guests. Everything about Marcus, Zara, and Gray came across as desperate and performative. They needed to be liked and adored. But my Violet...she couldn't even help but be every bit of herself at all times, whether she was quietly digesting conversation around her, or smirking at the response on the tip of her lips that she knew better than to speak aloud.

The Violet that I'd first brought to my family's New Year's party over a year ago had been so worried about belonging, but I'd seen such a shift in her. She didn't even have to try to belong, because she no longer needed the external validation, but also because she did belong...with me.

I almost envied how effortless she made it look, even though I knew how hard she'd worked with Dr. Short to process her feelings. I'd spent the first twenty years of my life fighting to feel worthy of people like Gray and Zara. Even now, I was holding my tongue instead of speaking my mind, falling back on the quiet persona I'd crafted to protect myself while I was growing up.

But when I was with Violet...she gave me strength of character I didn't even know I possessed. With her, it was impossible to retreat completely, because I needed to stay present for her. So often I found the world fading away when in her presence. I hadn't believed that soulmates were something that existed before I'd met her. But I felt it in every fiber of my being, that she filled in every crack in my psyche, broken by years of unworthiness. However cliche it might be, she completed me.

So when Amanda excused herself early from dinner, with an apology for not feeling well, I took that as my cue to follow suit. If my sister could escape her own ill-fated dinner party, I was happy to take advantage of the opportunity as well, whisking Violet upstairs, where we barely made it inside the door before combusting.

7

VIOLET

The second the door closed, Chance had me up against the wall, his hardness pressed against my stomach as his lips crashed into mine, furious and heated and desperate.

"Did you enjoy making me jealous?" he snarled, lips nipping and sucking as his hands pulled me closer, his hips rolling into me.

"You fucking love it," I taunted, sinking my teeth into his shoulder, but not hard enough to break skin.

"Did you like being bratty with a bunch of rich snobs?" he continued, sucking the pulse point at the juncture of my neck and shoulder, his fingers tangling in my hair, tugging.

"They're awful." I groaned as he yanked the cups of my dress down, exposing my breasts. Leaning down, he scooped me up, hauling me into his arms, bringing my chest to the level he wanted. I wrapped my legs around his hips for purchase, thankful for the wall at my back to keep me upright. Luckily the lace of the dress had a bit of stretch to it, allowing it to ride up my hips, exposing my bare sex.

"Hold on tight, muse," he crooned before that smart mouth of his latched on to one of my nipples, taking a strong pull. I let my head tip back against the wall, a moan escaping as he devoured me.

"It's not fair," I panted.

"What's not?" He peered up at me through his lashes, heat coursing through me at the sight of his desire.

"You've been winding me up all night," I whined.

"You need me, baby?"

I nodded, feeling my clit throb at just the thought of what he might do next.

"You'll have to wait." He smirked. "You've done this to yourself."

"Chance..." I groaned. The way he had me positioned, there was no way I'd be able to access his zipper to get to what I really wanted.

"Too bad." He glared before taking the other nipple in his mouth and sucking hard.

For far too long, he merely ground against me, not providing the friction I so desperately needed, all while lighting the rest of my body on fire. He'd never made me come without touching my pussy, even briefly, and I wondered if tonight he'd find a way.

I felt the slow heat of my climax as it crept up on me, inching forward at a crawl as he used his mouth to kiss and lick and suck every bit of bare skin he could find. I must have begun to whimper against him because finally he put me out of my misery, ending the teasing torture he'd so been enjoying.

"Have you learned your lesson?" His voice was low and rough.

"Yes," I panted.

Without letting me separate from the wall, he reached between us to pull his cock out, sheathing it inside me with one stroke.

I cried out, the pressure sharp but exquisite.

"You knew exactly what you were doing," Chance accused as he plunged in and out, taking me hard and fast.

"I wanted to push you," I keened.

"You wanted me to suffer," he growled.

"Only a little," I simpered.

As if to scold me, his next thrust was particularly deep. I could only melt against him, my eyes rolling back into my head as I let the ecstasy pulse through me.

He continued at a punishing pace, his lips returning to my neck, sucking so hard I knew he'd leave a mark, right where anyone could see it. That was exactly what he wanted...for everyone to know who I belonged to.

Without warning, my climax crested. I held tight as I spasmed against him. He took a moment to adjust me in his arms before continuing to piston inside me, needing only another few pumps before his pace became erratic and he was grunting into my neck as he spilled inside of me.

"You okay, sweetheart?" he whispered, cutting through our heavy breathing as we both slowly returned to earth.

I nodded against him, a smile on my lips. "I'm never wearing panties again."

Chance chuckled darkly.

"The lights aren't working," I mumbled, still half-asleep as I flipped the light switch in the bathroom back and forth with no luck.

"That's weird." Chance sat up in bed, rubbing the sleep from his eyes.

His dark hair fell over his forehead, and I bit my lip as moments of the night before flashed in my mind. Chance behind me while I was on my hands and knees—him lapping between my thighs—beneath me as I rode him. I'd never tire of the insatiable passion he ignited inside me.

Momentarily distracted by the bare muscled planes of his chest in the dim morning light, I shook my head, refocusing on the issue at hand.

I walked over to the bedroom light switches next to the door, and sure enough, those weren't working either.

Frowning, I crossed the room to the large window, parting the curtains to reveal a dreary ocean view, as rain pelted the glass and dark clouds loomed outside, casting the once-blue ocean in shadow, causing the water to appear just as dark and threatening as the weather above.

"Amanda said something about a storm coming in at dinner last night. I bet it knocked the power out," I commented.

Chance eyed me lasciviously as he leaned back against the headboard. "Then come back to bed if we're stuck here."

"You might have worn me out last night." I laughed, ignoring the pleasant soreness between my legs, my favorite reminder of how much I had enjoyed his attention.

"I doubt it." He opened his arms, beckoning me toward him.

But before I could take a step, my stomach growled loud enough for him to hear.

His brows knit together, a frown marring his handsome face. "Okay, coffee and breakfast first. Then back to bed."

I nodded in agreement, hoping that we could scrounge up something, even without the power.

Thankfully, after we'd dressed and gone downstairs, we found everyone gathered in the kitchen and breakfast nook. Seeing coffee mugs and plates scattered amongst the group set my stomach growling again.

Chance's warm hand was at the small of my back as we approached everyone.

"My followers are going to be so worried about me." Zara shook her head in frustration. She was wearing a matching workout set in light brown, her auburn hair pulled up into a high ponytail. Arms crossed over her chest and lips pursed, you would have thought her world was coming to an end. "My hormones are going to be off all day without my regular genmaicha."

I'd never heard of genmaicha before, and I almost wondered if she'd made it up to sound more cultured.

"I'm sorry about your tea, Zara," Hiram apologized from the kitchen, where he was helping Ruth with an expensive-looking espresso machine.

Gray glared at Zara, annoyed that she was complaining to their host and his potential investor.

“Thank goodness I made sure to include multiple generators in the planning,” Marcus called out from the living room couch where he was lounging with a thick book in hand and a mug resting precariously on the edge of the coffee table.

“The lights are out upstairs,” I told Hiram when he made eye contact with me. I hadn’t meant to cause him stress, but I wasn’t sure if he knew.

“The generators only power critical systems and areas like the kitchen and utilities so they last longer.” He sighed.

Gray stood from the dining nook banquette and began wandering around the living room, holding his phone up, trying to get a signal, I guessed.

“If the power’s out, the cellular networks will be as well,” Hiram told Gray. “They’re already spotty out here to begin with.”

Gray shook his head, ignoring Hiram’s assessment as he followed the line of the windows.

“Too bad nobody’s invented a startup to control the weather,” Marcus joked, crossing one leg over the other, almost seeming to enjoy Gray’s annoyance at the situation. “We’re stuck. No use being angry about it. It’ll clear eventually.”

"Stuck?" Chance cocked his head at Marcus.

"Bridge is washed out," Hiram answered his question. "Only the third time since it was built seventy years ago."

I glanced out the floor-to-ceiling windows at the grey horizon, rain still pounding against the house. Swallowing thickly, I hoped it wouldn't be closed for too long. I wasn't sure how long I could stomach being trapped with Amanda's guests.

The sound of the espresso machine filled the space. "Coffee, Miss?" Ruth asked me, her temperament harried as she darted a nervous glance over to Zara, who glared at the half-eaten muffin on her plate.

"I'll take whatever is easiest," I told her. "Even instant, if you have hot water." The last thing I wanted to do was make more work for the girl, who had her hands full.

"I can make it if you point me in the right direction," Chance offered from behind me.

Ruth's shoulders fell slightly, relief evident on her face as she realized Chance and I would be much easier to please than the others. "I'll put a kettle on," she told us as she retrieved a jar of instant coffee from a cabinet, setting it on the counter.

Chance pulled out one of the barstools at the kitchen island for me before making his way into the kitchen to help Ruth and Hiram. "You doing okay, man?" Chance asked Hiram as he plucked a pastry from a box and put it on a plate before sliding it across the counter to me.

I took a brief moment to swoon. He always made sure I was taken care of first...in more ways than one.

"Yeah, just need a little bit of quiet," Hiram replied, quiet enough that the others couldn't hear.

"Where's Amanda?" I asked, taking a bite of the pastry.

"Upstairs," Hiram said as he rinsed a component of the espresso machine under the faucet. "She's not feeling well."

Chance and I frowned at the same time, hating the thought of our lovely Amanda not feeling her best, especially while being forced to entertain guests.

"I'll go check on her," I said.

I was about to pop out of the chair when Chance stopped me. "Have some coffee first, then we'll go up."

I gave him a nod. He knew I'd be cranky if I didn't get some caffeine in me soon.

Chance sidled up next to me as we waited for the water to boil. "Sorry our first day is going to be confined inside," he murmured through a bite of his own food.

"Honestly, I wouldn't mind." I paused, shooting a glance at

Zara and Gray, who were arguing under their breaths across the breakfast banquette. "If it was just family."

He gave a knowing chuff.

"I could read all day on the couch and you could feed me grapes by hand." I winked at him.

"Oh?" He perked up, a laugh on the tip of his lips. "Is that a fantasy you have?"

"Maybe." I shrugged. "I also need to take a ride on their rolling library ladder before I leave."

That got a solid snort from him. "Definitely."

"You know I'm not that hard to please," I remarked.

Chance raised an eyebrow.

I shoved him. His grin widened as he banded his arm around my waist, pulling me and my stool closer to him in the process.

Sure I was particular, but I had simple tastes at the end of the day.

We ate breakfast in a comfortable silence between the two of us, his thigh pressed against mine below the counter. He always needed to be connected to me, and I loved how unabashedly affectionate he was. But although the two of us were quiet, it only made Zara, Gray, and Marcus seem that much louder.

Zara had moved on to complain about having to rebook their tickets to Ibiza, directly from the local airport, for a third time. "They'd better not charge us when we don't show up this afternoon. It's not my fault we don't have power or internet service."

Marcus called to her from across the room, assuring her that he knew someone who worked as a concierge at the airport that would make sure she was taken care of.

All while Gray continued to sneak sips from a flask, while he wandered around the large space looking for a signal, seeming to think his actions were going unnoticed.

But I noticed.

"Upstairs?" Chance asked, leaning in to kiss my cheek.

"I'll go." I slipped out of the barstool. "Why don't you stay down here and make sure Hiram doesn't have a breakdown."

Chance glanced over at Hiram and Ruth, who were still trying to get the espresso machine working. "Alright."

I knocked softly on Amanda and Hiram's bedroom door before entering, just in case she was sleeping. But a moment later, I heard a soft "come in."

"Good morning." I smiled, handing her the tea Ruth had asked me to bring up.

"Hey," she replied, pushing up on her hands to sit up in the bed.

"Are you okay, Amanda? You weren't yourself at dinner last night either." I sat down on the edge of the bed, setting down the borrowed headband I'd retrieved from my room to return it to her.

She released a heavy sigh. "I'm pregnant."

My eyes shot open.

"Amanda!" I lunged forward to hug her.

She let me pull her in close, but when she tensed a moment later, I released her.

"Fuck," she muttered, swinging her legs out of the bed and dashing for the bathroom. Moments later, the sounds of retching followed.

When it seemed the nausea had subsided, I peeked in through the doorway, finding Amanda slumped next to the toilet. "The morning sickness might kill me," she grumbled.

"Oh, Amanda," I commiserated. Pulling a water bottle from the counter, where I suspected Hiram had placed it for her, I knelt down next to her and handed it to her. "I'm sorry you're sick."

She reclined against the cabinets, taking a swig of the water. "I can't keep anything down. But Ruth found a ginger tea that's been helping."

"I just brought up some for you." I nodded toward the bedroom. "How far along?"

"Almost the end of the first trimester."

I looked down at her stomach, but she was wearing an oversized tee, so I couldn't see a bump.

Sensing my appraisal, she switched topics. "You're not wearing one of your outfits."

I glanced at my own attire. I'd thrown on the same outfit I'd worn yesterday for travel, just a pair of leggings and one of Chance's oversized hoodies. "I'll change," I grumbled.

Amanda smiled. "Try the deep purple set. It'll feel like you're wearing sweats."

I laughed at her tenacity. "You gonna be okay?"

She nodded. "The doctor said it could go away any day or stick around the whole time. Everyone is different. So fuck me, right?"

We shared a laugh.

"I'm glad it's not something more serious," I admitted.

"Oh, it's very serious." She smiled in jest. "You're going to be an auntie. Are you ready for that responsibility? I'll expect you and Chance to teach the baby how sarcasm works and all your tips on being the most stubborn woman alive."

I let my jaw drop. "I'm not *that* stubborn."

She leveled me with a glare.

"Maybe a little stubborn," I said through clenched teeth.

"Chance also needs to give them swimming lessons."

"And what will you and Hiram be imparting to the baby?"

"Obviously my fashion sense, impeccable taste, and society savvy." She tsked, as if it was the most obvious answer in the world. "And Hiram has everything else: social skills, intelligence, financial advice."

I could only giggle in response. "The kid sounds covered."

Amanda beamed at me, then glanced down at her belly. "I'm scared, but I'm so excited."

"You're going to be amazing," I reassured her. "Do your parents know?"

"Mom does. I'm not sure if she told Dad, but he hasn't said anything. He's been wrapped up closing a big acquisition."

I schooled my features. While Chance had made some headway toward civility with his father, and me agreeing to sign a prenup had certainly helped with that progress, I hated that both Chance and his sister remained such an afterthought for him, next to his work.

"Do you know if it's a boy or a girl?"

Amanda shook her head. "Hiram wants it to be a surprise, but I don't think there's any world in which I could wait." She looked up at me through her lashes. "If it's a girl, I want to name her Mitzi."

I felt my lips tremble and eyes fill with tears at the thought. Although I'd never met their grandmother Mitzi, I felt very connected to her, especially after what we'd discovered at Harper House over the holidays. "Maybe Sasha for a boy," I suggested.

"Maybe." She smiled down at her stomach. "But I think she's a girl."

I hoped she was.

Taking a deep breath, Amanda reached out for my hand. "I'm feeling better. Help me up so I can go drink some of that tea."

I obliged, keeping a grip on her as she walked back toward the bed.

"Oh! Let's put the headband away quick." She snagged it from the bed, shaking me off as she made her way to the closet on her own.

I followed a few steps behind, patiently waiting as she unlocked the hidden safe.

"What the fuck!?" she gasped.

I stepped up behind her to see what was wrong, only to find that the safe, once full of sparkling vintage jewelry, was empty.

8

VIOLET

"Something happened upstairs. Amanda needs you," I whispered urgently to Hiram.

His eyes went wide. "Is it the b—" He stopped himself, but I knew what he'd meant to say.

Chance glanced between the two of us, brows knit, trying to figure out what was going unspoken.

"They're both fine, but she needs you upstairs," I told him.

Chance's gaze cut to mine, a silent question in his expression, perhaps wondering if he'd interpreted my implication correctly.

The three of us headed back upstairs to find Amanda. I didn't miss the fact that Gray, Zara, and Marcus were all watching us cautiously, but the latter two at least had the decency to pretend like they weren't. Gray's eyes followed us with wary curiosity until we were out of sight. And Ruth was nowhere to be found.

Upstairs, Hiram rushed to his bedroom, Chance and I followed in his wake.

The moment he opened the door, Amanda burst into tears. He knelt before where she sat at the edge of the bed and pulled her into his arms, speaking softly with words of comfort.

"It has to be a mistake," she sobbed. "They can't be gone. They're all I had left of her." I knew she meant her grandmother. My heart ached for her. I'd never known any of my grandparents, but Amanda and Chance felt such a bond with Mitzi.

"What happened?" Chance asked, looking between me and Amanda.

"The safe's empty," I told him, "Someone took all of Amanda's jewelry—your grandma's pieces."

His lips parted in surprise.

"It's all priceless—irreplaceable," Amanda cried.

All the color had drained from Chance's face. "That's not—but we were here—everything was there last night," he stuttered before pacing over to the walk-in closet.

I was hot on Chance's heels, watching as he swung open the safe and turned to me, absolutely stunned. "How did this happen?"

I shook my head, still in shock myself.

He pushed past me, walking back into the bedroom. "We need to call the police right now."

"The lines are down." Hiram's jaw ticked.

"Don't you have a satellite phone or a ham radio or something?" Chance said frantically.

Hiram pursed his lips while Amanda continued to cry on his shoulder.

"Who would do this?" She hiccuped.

Who indeed.

"It's our property. I could demand to search everyone's rooms," Hiram suggested.

"Nobody would ever come visit us again," Amanda wailed.

"Baby, we have to do something," he tried.

"I'll talk to them." Amanda pushed off the bed, but stumbled with her first step.

Thankfully Hiram was next to her and caught her easily. "You are staying in bed, like the doctor told you to." His voice was commanding. I hadn't heard him be so direct with her. "You are not allowed to endanger yourself or the baby."

Chance drew in a sharp breath.

Amanda's gaze flickered to his. "Surprise," she said, her tone deadpan.

"You're really pregnant?" he asked, his voice softening upon confirming the news.

"I hoped to tell you under better circumstances. I've already given Violet a list of your duties and responsibilities."

Chance stepped toward the bed, reaching out to hold Amanda's hand. "I know how much those pieces meant to you, but they're not more valuable than your health."

Amanda frowned, her eyes refilling with tears.

"We'll figure out what happened," I declared.

Everyone in the room turned to look at me.

"We will?" Chance asked.

"Well, we'll try," I corrected. "You stay up here and rest. Chance and I will go downstairs and see what we can glean from the others."

Chance gave a slow nod, hesitantly agreeing with my plan.

"Nobody's left the house since the safe was full. That jewelry is still here somewhere." I stated what we surely all had to be thinking. "And if it's here, I think we can find it."

I wasn't sure if I believed what I was saying, but I wanted to.

"When was the last time you accessed the safe?" Chance asked Amanda.

"Last night, before dinner, when I lent Violet the headband," she replied, giving Chance an oddly pointed look.

He audibly swallowed.

"And you locked it properly?" I cut in.

Amanda's gaze swung to me. "I thought so." She shrugged.

"When would they have had an opportunity?" Chance looked at me first, then back to Amanda and Hiram.

"Before dinner. We were alone in the dining room for a while," Hiram offered.

"I've been sleeping terribly and was up sick half the night, so it's unlikely they would have been able to come in after then without being detected," Amanda admitted, worry etched on her face at the thought of someone being in her bedroom while she lay sleeping and vulnerable.

"And we discovered it empty at"—I looked down at my watch—"9:20 a.m." Counting backward a few minutes to factor in having gone downstairs to get Chance and Hiram. "That gives us a timeline."

"It's been over fourteen hours since dinner. Someone easily could have come and gone in that time." Hiram shook his head. I could tell he didn't think there was a possibility of recovering anything, even with the storm cutting us off.

But I wasn't so sure.

"The chef left," Chance said, glancing at me.

"But he was never outside the kitchen. When we came down early for dinner I could see him working through the dining room door leading to the kitchen the whole night," Amanda told us. "He was even packing up when I left dinner early. I walked him to the door before heading upstairs."

"So we assume it happened in the, what? Thirty-minute window after you gave me the headband, before everyone arrived for dinner. So we should focus on the four people who weren't downstairs early," I asserted.

"Three," Amanda corrected.

I cocked my head.

"Ruth would never," she insisted.

"We need to consider everyone," Chance told her softly. "She knew about the safe. She was up in the room when it was open, while you were showing Violet the pieces."

"She wouldn't though." Amanda shook her head. "She's practically family." She spared a glance to Hiram, whose jaw was clenched. "Marcus knew about the safe too. He helped decide on the positioning and even the make and model, based on what his other clients use."

"What about Zara and Gray?" I asked.

Amanda looked down, her cheeks going pink. "Zara complimented a pair of earrings I was wearing when she first arrived and I told her about my vintage collection."

"Is that what Gray told you to sell?" Hiram asked.

Amanda nodded. "He said a collection like that would go for a pretty penny at auction, but I told them everything had enormous sentimental value, and I'd never part with a single piece." Her eyes bounced to the solitaire necklace at my throat, a piece which she had relinquished to Chance to gift to me. The implication was clear. She wouldn't part with anything, except in extraordinary circumstances.

"So they didn't know about the safe exactly, but they knew about the collection." I sighed.

"They might as well have." She huffed. "Everyone I know has a safe. And the closet is the first place they'd check. But what about the biometric lock? It's hardwired into the house to prevent something like this from happening. I just don't understand how they got in."

"Maybe they got your fingerprint off a glass using some tape," I blurted out without thinking.

Chance shook his head. "I don't know if that kind of thing works outside of movies."

I pursed my lips.

"I want to look at the safe one more time, and then we'll go downstairs and see what we can figure out," Chance redirected the conversation.

"And I'm forced to sit up here like a useless baby incubator," Amanda complained.

Hiram released a beleaguered breath, but Chance and I were already halfway to the closet.

"You shouldn't have promised her anything," Chance muttered the moment we crossed the threshold.

"We solved multiple murders last year and discovered a secret room at your parents' estate that had been hidden for decades, all without any help. I think we can figure out which of the three numbskulls downstairs did this." I stuck my tongue out at him.

"I just don't want to get Amanda's hopes up." He took my hand, giving it a gentle squeeze.

"I don't want to either, but I also don't want her crying up here all day thinking the jewelry is gone forever. We can ask a few questions while we wait for the weather to clear," I reasoned.

He released a deep exhale.

"You know I'm right."

"Just a few questions," he relented.

"Just a few." I grinned, pleased to have gotten my way.

Chance stood, staring at the open safe, hands on hips.

"What are we looking for exactly?" I asked him.

"Amanda's right, they shouldn't have been able to get in without her fingerprints." He crouched, examining the seam around the safe, where it was slotted into the wall. "Do you have your cell, baby? I left mine in the room." He held out a hand.

I dug in my pocket and handed it to him, watching as he entered my passkey and turned on the flashlight.

After everything that had happened the year before at Montgomery, there was an exceedingly high level of trust between Chance and me. He'd saved my life, after all. So what did cell phone passwords matter? Neither of us had anything to hide, but we knew if something happened to either of us, it could be the difference between life or death, so it wasn't a problem utilizing full transparency with one another.

"No damage that I can see. Which means they had to have gone in through the lock." He continued to examine the safe, looking for any indication of tampering.

"The keypad still has power, so the hardwire wasn't cut or it has backup battery power," I observed. I reached out to touch the keypad, but Chance stopped me.

"You should leave it. We don't want to mess up evidence the police might need," he reasoned.

One thing was clear to me: this hadn't been a crime of opportunity. It had been planned and executed very precisely.

Whoever took Amanda's jewelry knew exactly what they were doing. And in my gut, I knew the thief was sitting downstairs, watching the clock tick down, thinking they'd gotten away with it.

Whoever did this was a fool to think I'd let them leave unscathed.

9

CHANCE

I gave Violet's hand a squeeze as we rounded the corner from the entryway back into the open kitchen and living room.

Since the moment I'd seen the empty safe for myself, I'd had a pit in my stomach.

Violet's engagement ring was in that safe, and she didn't even know it was among the items that had gone missing. I knew she wouldn't blame me, but she'd be devastated nonetheless. Just like the rest of the pieces from my grandmother, it was irreplaceable.

The others were all awkwardly awaiting news of what had happened, as it had been obvious something was wrong when we'd gone upstairs to talk to Amanda.

Ruth was still fiddling with the espresso machine, but cast a wary glance toward us as I pulled out the same barstool as before for Violet to sit on.

Marcus had propped himself up against the arm of the couch to watch everything unfold.

Gray and Zara were seated awkwardly at the dining nook in the corner. The more she leaned away from him, the more he inched forward, much to her dismay.

The whole group started when a loud clap of thunder sounded overhead. Wind and rain were still lashing the floor-to-ceiling windows, making the room feel even more on edge.

"Is Amanda okay?" Marcus finally broke the verbal silence.

Violet and I turned to regard him, then shared a look before Violet responded. "She's okay," she started hesitantly. "But she's discovered her safe has been emptied of her priceless jewelry collection."

Zara's loud and theatrical gasp sounded over the rain a moment before Ruth dropped the machine piece she was holding, the metal clanging on the counter.

Marcus's face paled as his whole posture seemed to stiffen.

And Gray laughed.

All eyes shot to him, surprised by his reaction.

"What!?" He guffawed.

Zara's glare was deadly.

"You can't be serious." He looked around the room at all the eyes on him. "I hope you don't think one of us had anything to do with it."

"Of course not," Zara cut in. "This exact thing happened to my good friend Tay—well, I'm sure she wouldn't want me spreading rumors, but it was discovered to be her assistant." She cut a hard glare at Ruth, who withered under the attention. "Can you imagine!? It's always those you least expect and trust the most."

Violet grumbled something that sounded suspiciously like a string of creative expletives under her breath. I squeezed her waist in acknowledgement.

"The safe was top-of-the-line." Marcus sat up completely, draping his frame over the back of the sectional where he was stationed. "It should have been impenetrable except via biometric scan."

"Don't they use Davis Security Systems too?" Gray pointed out. "They're the best of the best. They don't even take on clients under a certain income threshold."

I'd never heard of Davis Security Systems, but I found it interesting that Gray knew of them, enough to have noticed they were the company Amanda and Hiram used.

"Once the power is back on, Hiram should be able to help you access the security logs for the property," Ruth suggested quietly.

"Are there any cameras?" Violet asked her.

"Not upstairs." Ruth shook her head.

"This is ridiculous," Zara proclaimed. "Poor Amanda. Who would do such a thing!?" Her overture felt performative at best.

"Once they've been able to reconnect with outside communication, Hiram plans to notify the police. It's likely you may need to remain at the house until they arrive, in case they have any questions."

"We have a flight."

"I have investor meetings."

"You have no authority to detain us."

Zara, Gray, and Marcus argued at the same time.

Ruth remained silent in the corner of the kitchen.

"I assumed you'd all want to stay to clear your names," Violet spoke up. "An incident like this could follow even the most well-respected person. Could you imagine what the press would spin?" She looked directly at Zara when she made her last point.

I took a moment to admire Violet. She was always so determined and focused when she set her mind to something. I knew it stemmed from the need for hyper-independence as a child due to her mother's depression, but I often found myself in awe of Violet's mind. She saw right through people to their innermost insecurities and goals.

Zara sputtered, as if she'd been personally victimized by Violet's statement.

"I think we all know where we should be looking." Gray folded his arms over his chest, looking anywhere but Ruth, his intended target.

"If you think of anything you heard or saw that might help Amanda, please let us know," I told the group, utilizing my most authoritative teacher voice, knowing it likely wouldn't work on the crowd before me.

"And sometimes people make mistakes." I tried to sound nonchalant. "If the jewelry turns up, there'd be no reason to contact the police." It was a long shot that whoever had gone to all that trouble would give in so easily, but I had a feeling being trapped in the house due to inclement weather hadn't been part of their plan. Anything was worth a shot.

"I need to meditate." Zara pushed out from the dining nook. "This is all just too much." She promptly stormed off past the kitchen toward the spa and yoga studio.

"I'll be in the library reading through my investor reports." Gray huffed, marching across the living room in the opposite direction of his wife.

Marcus just shook his head and resumed reading on the couch.

Violet slipped off the barstool and rounded the kitchen island to help Ruth reassemble the espresso machine.

"I'll answer whatever questions you want," Ruth told Violet quietly as she pulled another tea bag from the cabinet. "Can I check on Amanda first?"

Violet nodded, giving the girl a brief pat on the arm before glancing over her shoulder at me, then walking toward the dining room, where we could talk without worrying that Marcus could hear us.

"So that was weird, right?" Violet's hands landed on her hips the moment we were alone.

"I would have thought they'd want to be more helpful," I agreed.

Violet leaned against the credenza, crossing one leg over another.

I must have looked upset, because she reached out to twine her fingers through mine. "Hey, it'll be okay," she attempted to comfort me. "In a weird way, their shady reactions make things easier. It's suspicious as fuck." She cocked her head, curling the edges of her lips as she squeezed my hand. "So don't worry, okay?"

I felt my chest tighten. I knew at that moment, it was now or never to come clean.

"There's something I need to tell you," I admitted softly.

Violet's expression tensed, but she said nothing as her eyes studied me intently.

"Your ring was in the safe."

"What ring?" she asked, confused. Pulling her hand from mine, she raised it between us. "My ring's fine."

I gulped. "That's not your ring," I confessed.

"What?"

"It needed to be resized, but you didn't want to part with it. And now it's missing and it's my fault." I got it all out as fast as I could, not wanting to leave anything else between us... other than the secret elopement I was planning, that was.

Her jaw clenched, then her lips parted. They closed again. She seemed to be at a loss for words, which was always a bad thing when it came to my Violet.

I awaited her wrath in silent dismay.

"I need you to start from the beginning," she said finally. "I don't understand."

Taking a deep breath, I did as instructed. "You'd mentioned to me several times that the ring was a little big and that you wanted to get it resized—that you were worried about it slipping off," I began. "But when I suggested we have a jeweler fix it, you said you didn't want to part with it. That you didn't trust anyone with the ring."

She nodded slowly, remembering the conversations we'd had.

"So I thought I'd surprise you."

She frowned so deeply I had to suppress a laugh, given the serious nature of our discussion.

"Amanda helped me find a reputable jeweler who worked on vintage pieces. I had him make a replica of your ring"—I motioned to the fake on her left hand—"and I swapped them a few weeks ago. I sent him your ring to be resized and just got it back. I was going to return the real ring to you while we were here. I asked Amanda to store it in her safe so you didn't find it in the room." I slightly rearranged some facts to suit my needs.

Violet took a measured breath as she centered herself. She glanced down at the ring again, examining it. "I thought the center stone looked duller than usual, but I figured I wasn't doing a good enough job of cleaning it."

"I'm sorry, Violet." I took a step toward her, needing her reassurance.

She looked up at me, tears welling in her eyes. "It's not your fault." Her voice warbled.

I felt my throat go tight at the sound. I knew I never could have predicted what would happen, but I still felt like I had failed her somehow.

But in the next moment, she closed the distance between us, wrapping her arms around my waist and burying her head against my chest. I pulled her in tighter. "I'm so sorry, baby," I whispered.

"I'm not leaving this house without my ring," she growled against me, her words laced with determination and spite, even through her tears.

10

Violet

Hell hath no fury like Violet Price scorned.

Whoever took my fucking engagement ring was going to pay for their indiscretion. I hadn't decided how yet, and the method might depend on the culprit, but I'd make sure they'd regret what they'd done for a long, long time.

"So what's our plan?" I asked Chance. My chest was tight with anger. I was going to do whatever it took to recover Amanda's jewelry. "How are we going to suss out who did this?"

"What do we know?" Chance asked. "Facts only. No conjecture. Means. Motive. Opportunity."

I narrowed my gaze at him. What he meant was that he didn't

want my side commentary about how awful Amanda's guests were.

Fine.

I'd complain about them after I had my ring back.

"The safe was most likely looted in the half hour between Amanda leaving the room before dinner, and when the guests arrived," I started. "As far as we know, all four of them had the opportunity to sneak upstairs in that window. Any of them could have somehow figured out how to open the safe, but Marcus and Ruth appear to have had the most knowledge about the safe itself."

"And motive?"

"Unclear," I replied. "We haven't interacted enough to ascertain motive, although maybe Amanda has more information."

"That's okay. Then that's what we focus on when we talk to them," Chance decided. "We can start with simple questions like where they were, if they saw anything—make them feel like we're not even considering them, just that we want their help finding the person who did this."

I nodded. It was a great angle, and one we'd both used on our students if they were being particularly difficult.

"Maybe if we ask them why someone would do it, the perpetrator will tell on themselves?" I tried.

Chance snorted a laugh. "I don't know if we'll get that lucky, but you never know."

"I'll probably have to corner Gray by myself, and I'd imagine you'd have better luck with Marcus on your own." He grimaced.

"You'd let me talk to Marcus alone?" I teased, tugging at the zipper on his sweater.

Chance's eyes darkened. "If he tries anything..."

I merely laughed, pushing up on my toes to plant a kiss on his lips.

"What about Zara and Ruth?" he redirected the conversation.

"I'll take Zara. I deal with moms like her at school all the time," I offered. "Maybe let's see if we can find Ruth first and we can talk with her together. She seems to know this house like the back of her hand, and she's been dealing with the guests for a few days. She's bound to have learned something useful."

I turned to leave, but Chance gently grabbed my wrist to stop me. I glanced back at him in question.

"You know we can't rule Ruth out, right? I know Amanda and Hiram trust her, and I don't want it to have been her either, but we need to remain open to all possibilities," he reminded me.

I swallowed hard, but gave him a firm nod.

It didn't take long to find Ruth. She was working on folding laundry in the back utility room. She jumped when I gently knocked on the doorframe to get her attention. Clearly her nerves were shot from the whole ordeal.

She wore the same outfit as the day before, likely her uniform, of a simple black tee and black slacks. Her curly hair was pulled up into a messy bun and the bags under her eyes were more pronounced in the dimmer emergency lighting of the utility room.

"Hey, do you have a minute?" I asked softly, casting a glance around the spotless space. Obviously Ruth was proficient at her job, as every space within Amanda's home appeared nothing less than pristine.

Ruth's gaze ping-ponged between me and Chance for a moment before she agreed. "Sure, as long as I can keep working."

"Of course," I nodded. "Can I help you?"

She glanced up, her eyebrows high at the offer. "No—no, that's alright," she stuttered. "Thank you though."

Chance leaned against the countertop farthest from Ruth, perhaps not wanting to intimidate her.

"Is it okay if we ask you about last night?" I started. I didn't want her to feel like she had to comply, but I hoped she and the rest of our suspects understood what any lack of cooperation would communicate on their behalf.

"Of course, whatever I can do to help. Stress is the last thing Amanda needs." She glanced up to give Chance and me a knowing look.

"Talk to me about what your evening was like last night," I requested.

"I was all over the place," she began. "And before you ask, I don't have anyone to vouch for my whereabouts for the whole time." She frowned. "Both of you arrived while I was preparing the kitchen for the chef, per his instructions, since he was on a tight cooking timeline for the meal. He asked me to prep some food and have a list of requested utensils and supplies out and ready. I greeted him when he arrived and showed him around the kitchen, then I let Amanda know when the food would be ready for the guests on his behalf. You were both there when that happened." She looked between us again.

I nodded in agreement.

"And after that?"

"I don't know." She shook her head. "I set everything up in the dining room, and the chef kept asking me questions, so it took longer than usual. I had to chill the wine Amanda wanted out, and get the chef a different set of serving plates, and find the proper glasses. I had a million things to take care of." Her voice began to waver and I could sense the defeat in her tone.

"If you were downstairs most of the time, maybe there will be security footage that can clear you, once the systems are back online," I suggested.

Ruth stopped folding, but her eyes were still planted on the clothes in front of her. "No matter what you say, I know the police are going to think it was me."

"Why?" Chance asked softly.

Ruth's gaze raised to meet his. "Because I've stolen stuff before. I have a record, and even did some time in a detention center."

"When you were younger?" I asked, making an assumption from her calling it a detention center, and not a jail.

"I was in and out of the foster system—that's how I met Hiram. We stayed with the same family for a while," she told us.

I hadn't known Hiram had been in the system.

"I was desperate and running with a bad crowd, and it was a mistake I've regretted ever since." She sighed. "I've been so happy here, but I should have known it was too good to be true." She blinked back tears.

"Amanda and Hiram know you didn't do this," I told her.

Chance cast me a wary glance. I knew he'd told me not to rule people out, and I couldn't guarantee it wasn't her, or that the police wouldn't see her as the most obvious suspect, but I felt her pain in my gut. She didn't have to share any of this with us. It was clear she was uncomfortable, and embarrassed. But it was also obvious how much she liked Amanda and Hiram.

I believed her.

"Thank you," she replied softly. I hoped the admission brought her some comfort.

"What about the others?" Chance asked. "Did you see or hear anything odd or out of character last night, or while they've been here?"

"Zara's usually in the spa, but when she's in her room, she would call down constantly to ask me to bring things up to her. We didn't have most of what she wanted, I still don't know what Manuka honey is." Ruth rolled her eyes. "And the second the chef arrived, she asked if he could make her a separate menu that was low-histamine and lectin-free. Like the guy had just walked in the door and the kitchen phone rang."

I snorted a laugh, picturing Zara's face pressed against the window, eagerly awaiting the chef's arrival to unleash her trending dietary restrictions on him.

"And the men?" Chance tried to keep us on track.

"Marcus read on the patio for most of the day, but he wasn't there when I was giving the chef a quick tour because I showed him the grill outside, in case he needed it, and I remember cleaning up the empty dishes he left behind. Gray took his calls out in the sunroom. He's always on the phone —always pacing around," she noted.

"But he was in Hiram's office for a while before you arrived yesterday. Their conversation seemed a little intense when I came to let him know you'd just pulled up. Hiram seemed happy about the interruption, but Gray was pissed. I don't know where he went after that, but I didn't see him downstairs until dinner.

I looked over at Chance. I wondered if he was thinking the same thing I was, that maybe they'd argued about Hiram not wanting to invest in his shifty company.

"Who do you think did it?" I decided to be bold.

Ruth's lips parted, her wide eyes meeting mine.

"Just between us," I clarified, my voice lower, softer.

She took a beat, her gaze darting nervously to Chance in the corner. "I think the couple did it."

"Zara and Gray?" I confirmed.

Ruth nodded.

"Why?"

"I swear I wasn't eavesdropping, I was just going to wipe down all of the machines, but I heard them arguing in the gym the night before you arrived," she relayed.

"Arguing about what?" I raised a brow. From my own observations, Zara had no patience for Gray, but she seemed more passive in her distaste.

"I didn't hear much, but Zara was screaming about all the money being gone and calling him a bunch of names."

"Not surprised," Chance echoed my sentiments exactly.

"Did you tell Hiram what you heard?" I asked, out of curiosity.

Ruth swallowed, then gave a slow nod. "He said he was never planning on investing with Gray, but after what I heard, he said he'd make sure to warn his associates away."

She looked down at the full hamper of clothes in front of her, then back to me. "I need to get back to work. Did you have any more questions for me?"

I glanced at Chance before shaking my head. "I'll let you know if I think of anything else. You've been a great help," I reassured her.

She gave me a small smile in response.

"If they're broke, some vintage jewelry would catch a pretty penny at auction," I repeated Amanda's words to Chance, bumping my hip into his as we made our way down the hall back toward the living room.

"Money is always one of the best motivators," he agreed. "If he isn't two sheets to the wind, maybe I can get more intel from Gray without him realizing what he's revealing.

"I'll see what our Z-list wellness guru knows." I grimaced.

After a quick change into the matching plum workout set Amanda had recommended, I made my way over to the spa. It seemed more of a combination of a bunch of things, with a sauna box in one corner, a treatment chair in another, and half the room covered in foam matting for meditation and yoga floorwork.

And that was where I found Zara Sable, legs crossed, hands perfectly pointed in a prayer position, not a hair out of place.

I took a moment to observe her from closer up. Her high ponytail pulled her skin back slightly. There were remnants of what was perhaps natural beauty at one point, but signs of both regular aging and cosmetic procedures detracted from who she probably had once been. Her tight brow, razor-sharp jawline, and large pillowy lips made her appear like so many other influencers. But I supposed as long as the work she'd had done made her happy, it shouldn't matter to me.

It was enough of a reminder of what kind of person Zara was to snap me back into the right mode for the subtle interrogation I'd need to complete. From what I could tell based on brief interactions I'd had and those I'd observed, Zara took advantage of others for a living. She acted like she was better than everyone else, but I had a suspicion she had an ego that was as fragile as glass. I'd need to handle her with kid gloves and make sure to throw in as much adoration and validation as I was capable of handling myself. That was the only way to get what I wanted from her.

Ready for the work ahead, I gently cleared my throat to get her attention without startling her.

Her eyes shot open, head snapping to regard me as I tried and failed to quietly close the door behind me. Gaze narrowed, she watched me cautiously as I made my way toward her. "What do you want?" She scowled.

Using my most sickly sweet teacher voice, I softened my expression when I knelt down beside her and said, "I just wanted to check and see if you were okay."

Her entire demeanor shifted when she thought I was coming to her as an ally. "Today has been just awful." She pouted. "I haven't been cut off from my followers for more than a few minutes, let alone hours. I can't even get them a message that I'm alive."

In my own twisted way, I thought it amusing that her not being able to monitor her likes and follows, in her mind, was more serious than what Amanda was going through.

I crossed my legs, sitting down next to her, angling my body toward hers. "At least you're warm, and in good company," I offered.

She snorted. "Hardly."

I raised a brow.

"Not Amanda and Hiram, they're lovely," she corrected herself. "The maid won't stop glaring at me, Gray's been—well, Gray"—she rolled her eyes—"and Marcus would rather read than talk through my design plans for the house. You'd think he'd want to secure another project."

"Why's that?" I asked casually, feigning indifference.

"Well, I shouldn't say, but his deceased wife's family has been going after him hard to contest the will." Zara batted her lashes, as if she was scandalized by just the idea of it all. "She left him everything. It was her money. She should've gotten to do what she wanted with it."

"But Marcus runs a successful architecture firm," I noted. "Or at least that's what Amanda said."

"Marcus has a pretty face and knows how to take care of a woman in the bedroom, but running a business is not his forte."

If I didn't know any better, I'd think from Zara's tone that she knew just how well Marcus seemed to take care of the women he bedded. I'd need to tuck that away for later.

"I've heard rumors of poor office management. Nobody wants to do their jobs these days. That maid acts like I've asked for the world when I need anything. It's not my fault Amanda wasn't prepared for company," she concluded.

I bit back a retort and instead said, "I think she was under the impression only Gray would be visiting. I'm sure she would have made prior accommodations if she'd known you were coming. All she's talked about is how much of an honor it's been to get to host you. She's a big fan of yours."

Zara preened. "Really? She didn't mention anything to me, but I suppose she'd want to be modest knowing I was staying here. That's kind of her."

"I'm sorry Gray hasn't made things easy for you." I pivoted the conversation slightly, unsure how protective she was of her husband, despite the fact that they seemed to be constantly bickering.

"Marriage is a trap," she sniped. "But it has its benefits."

I pressed my lips together to prevent harsh words.

"Amanda and Hiram seem to be doing pretty well."

"He does whatever she tells him to do, so I'm not surprised." She chuckled.

I didn't like her assessment of my soon-to-be sister- and brother-in-law. They were equally matched in character, intelligence, and values, and worked perfectly as a team. I wasn't sure why it bothered me so much that Zara thought their relationship was so one-dimensional.

"I hope Amanda's jewelry can be discovered before the police need to get involved." I was walking a fine line between ego-stroking and extracting information, but I needed to push a little harder to leave the conversation feeling like I'd at least tried. "You didn't happen to see or hear anything unusual before dinner, did you? I think everyone was scattered around the house."

"I was upstairs in my room doing my pre-dinner skincare routine. It's eleven steps and quite vigorous. I have a fourteen-part series on my social media doing a walk-through. You should check it out." Her eyes roamed over my face, appraising any imperfections she could find. "Really, I think it would help you."

"Thank you," I ground out, wondering if she'd had that answer out a little too quickly, as if she had been ready and waiting for me to ask.

"I know it's not polite to say, but they really should just search the maid's room for the jewelry and be done with it. I've seen this before. There's only one person on the property who needs the kind of money such a collection could bring."

I wasn't so sure about that, and Zara herself had just told me even Marcus might have a financial motive to take the jewels for himself.

"Maybe they will," I told her.

11

Violet

"Well aren't you a sight for sore eyes?" Marcus crooned the second I rounded the corner of the sofa, where he'd been lounging all day.

Long, lean legs, crossed over one another, his shoes up on the couch, which I found distasteful in a home where you were a guest, Marcus was the epitome of a lothario. As if to hammer his point home, his shirt was even unbuttoned far enough to show a hint of his sculpted chest.

Despite my disgust with him, even I had to admit he was a beautiful man, with his blonde hair and blue eyes giving him a Nordic sort of masculinity. I could see how he appealed to others, and although I saw through his charm, I recognized perhaps I was an exception to his magnetism.

"Does that really work for you?" I asked, plopping down on the opposite side of the couch. I'd never been one to enjoy men who were overtly flirtatious, although I supposed Chance had been an exception. The difference was that Chance never flirted with anyone else, just me. So it never felt as disingenuous as Marcus made it seem.

"I haven't met a woman I've pursued that hasn't succumbed to my charms." He flashed me a suggestive grin. "I think, given some time, and the proper...lubrication, I could bring you around." His double entendre made me cringe.

"I think I'd eat you alive." I gave him a saccharine smile.

"Maybe I'd eat you." He leaned forward, biting his lower lip.

I rolled my eyes through a laugh at his audacity. The thought of letting a man other than Chance near me made me sick.

"I'm well-tended to, thank you," I replied. "Shame about the weather." I switched topics, nodding at the window, where rain still hammered the outside of the home.

"I've been arguing with lawyers all week, so honestly, it's been a nice break not to have my phone going off every five minutes." He crossed his arms over his chest, flexing his biceps in the process. I was unsure if the move was intentional or not.

"Lawyers?" I questioned, already having a feeling I knew why, if Zara's gossip was true.

"Just a bunch of good-for-nothings that can't move on. Nothing for you to worry your pretty little head about, dear Violet."

"Zara mentioned there have been issues with your late wife's will." I took a chance to see how much I could push him.

"Well Zara should be using her mouth for much more pleasurable activities than spreading rumors about me," he said through his teeth, tension written clearly on his face.

"Sorry. She made it seem like it was common knowledge," I argued.

"I would have thought her and her gremlin of a husband have enough to deal with, rather than bother with me. But I suppose she's rather sour that I'm not as interested in her house project as she'd hoped," he spilled.

"Not enough of a challenge?" I raised a brow.

"Not enough in the piggy bank, I'm afraid." He chuckled. "For now anyway."

"Hmmm." I wondered how much he knew about their finances, but I got the sense he wouldn't share, even if he had the inside scoop. "You know I'd be remiss not to ask you about what happened this morning." I switched tactics and topics, getting to the heart of the matter.

"I suppose you would," he agreed, swinging his legs off the couch and scooting across the cushions toward me.

"Out of everyone in this house, you probably know the most about the safe," I stated.

"Nothing you couldn't look up online. But I only recommended it because it's the current gold standard for my level of clients. It should have been tamper proof, but I don't know enough about the technical specs to understand if it has any weaknesses." Marcus's tone came across as both defensive and resolute.

"And there was only the biometric lock?" I asked.

He shifted acutely. "Well, it has a master override combination in case the biometric pad fails, but Amanda would have set that code. I never knew what it was."

Curious.

That was the first I was hearing about the master override. I wondered why Amanda hadn't mentioned anything.

"I don't know what I can do or say to prove my innocence, but I can promise you I had nothing to do with this. I can't afford any bad press. If word got out that one of my clients had a security breach, it could bury me," he argued.

"Where were you last night before dinner?"

"On the patio reading. You saw me."

"After that," I clarified.

He sighed, his gaze falling from mine. “I was up in my room on calls. I’d been ignoring them for a couple hours, but Susan just kept calling non-stop, so I’d finally had enough.”

“Who’s Susan?” I asked.

He gave a mirthless chuckle. “My stepdaughter—Esme’s oldest child—fifty going on fifteen. She thinks she can talk me into ‘doing the right thing’ and relinquishing every penny I was given back to her and her mooching siblings, who’ve never worked a day in their lives and all married within society, so they don’t even need the money.” He glanced up at me. “They just don’t want me to have it.”

I swallowed. I believed him.

“If you had to place your bets, who’s our jewel thief?”

He pursed his lips before saying, “I suppose sweet, young Ruth has the most to gain, don’t you agree?”

I wasn’t so sure. And it wasn’t lost on me that Zara had said almost the same thing. Had they already spoken about the robbery and gotten their stories straight? Or were they just so entitled to assume that anyone below their station was the only likely suspect?

“We’ll find out,” I asserted.

Marcus’s expression turned grim.

"Tell me Gray confessed to everything like the dirtbag I'm pretty sure he is, and returned the jewels," I joked when Chance eventually wandered back up to our room, looking a little worse for the wear.

"I wish. He was useless. Spent the last two hours drunkenly rambling about how unfair it is that his business partner left him in the lurch on this project and that everyone who refused to give him capital funding is going to regret it when this is the next Silicon Valley Cinderella story."

Chance paced toward the bed, slipping off his shoes before crawling in next to me and laying his head in my lap.

"He can't wait to rub it in their faces. He made sure to say that last part like five times. He's really excited about showing them what a big mistake they made."

"Big mistake. Huge!" I laughed, quoting a famous movie line as I ran my fingers through his hair.

Chance chuckled with me. "What about your assignments?"

"Oh, ya know, they're both convinced Ruth did it because she's not one of them." I shook my head.

"Gray practically said the same thing," Chance relayed.

"Bunch of entitled rich assholes," I grumbled. "You'd think I'd be used to it by now between all the shit we deal with at school and your parents' society friends, but it still pisses me off. Every. Single. Time."

"I know, baby," Chance agreed.

"We should go talk to your sister and see what she thinks and how she wants us to proceed," I suggested.

"Alright," Chance sighed as he rose from the bed. I followed after him.

We managed to catch Hiram as he was entering their room with another steaming cup of tea for Amanda. "Hey," he greeted, holding the door open for us to enter before him.

Amanda was just where we'd left her that morning. Blonde hair up in a bun, makeup free, and in the same oversized tee, as she leaned up against the headboard. "Anything?" she asked, her brows lifting with hope.

"Nothing definitive." I shook my head. "But we've learned a bit more about your guests."

"Oh?" Hiram asked as he handed Amanda the tea.

"Marcus mentioned a master override code for the safe," I told Amanda. "He said he didn't know it, but that you would have set it up."

Her brow furrowed. "He never mentioned that to me. I just followed the instructions to load in fingerprints for me and Hiram."

I looked over to Chance. "Maybe that's how they got in?" I shrugged.

Chance looked uncertain.

"I don't think any of them have an alibi for the half hour before dinner, when we think the robbery happened," I told the group. "Unless Gray said something?"

Chance shook his head. "He said he was taking work calls around the house. He didn't get any more specific than that."

"Zara was upstairs moisturizing, Marcus said he was in his room on the phone as well, and Ruth was running around setting the table and helping the chef. The chef might be able to vouch for some of Ruth's time, and when the security cameras are back online, we might be able to track her movement downstairs and see if we can validate her claims," I relayed.

"What about motive?" Chance asked me. "Gray seems pretty hard up for cash, but he didn't say anything specific and he's drunk as a skunk, so not exactly a reliable source."

"I had a bit more luck. The money Marcus inherited from his late wife is being contested by her children, and Zara mentioned rumors about his firm not being run well, hinting that if his inheritance was revoked, he'd be in dire straits. Marcus confirmed the will being contested, but Zara's gossip is just conjecture at this point. He also revealed that this big house project Zara wants to work with him on isn't going to happen because she doesn't have the funding."

Amanda's brow furrowed. "I haven't had any issues with Marcus's firm. There hasn't been any indication about Zara and Gray's finances, other than his desperation for investors, but that's so common in our circles. It could be nothing, or everything."

I nodded in agreement.

"To add to that, they've been arguing all over the house. Hell, even Chance and I heard them fighting last night before dinner. Ruth too," I added, glancing at Hiram, knowing he had already been made aware of it. "Between the three of them, they're all still viable options, with means, motive, and opportunity."

"We need to figure out a way to make them crack." Chance sighed in frustration.

"There's something else," I hesitated before adding, "All three of your guests pointed the finger at Ruth."

"Of course they did," Hiram spit. "She's lived a hard life, much of it out of her own control. She is a good person, and she's trying so hard to get past the mistakes she made when she was younger."

"She mentioned her history," Chance chimed in. "She was up front about it all—almost defeated. I have a hard time believing she'd be so open about everything if she had something to do with the robbery."

"Exactly," Hiram agreed. "I mean we asked her to be the baby's nanny for fuck's sake. She needs stability and security. I know she wouldn't risk that. This feels completely set up to make her look guilty."

"We think so too," I spoke for myself and Chance. "But that's where our thief has made a mistake."

Amanda cocked her head.

"We should lean into it," I suggested. "We'll get Ruth on board, and pretend that she confessed or something and then the person who really did it will get comfortable. They might let something slip."

Hiram couldn't help but smile. "That's genius." He beamed.

But before we could say anything further, we heard yelling coming from outside in the hall. Chance and I exchanged a look of alarm before darting out to see what was going on. Hiram and Amanda were hot on our heels.

"We found something!" Zara exclaimed, crouching down next to another bedroom door on the opposite end of the hallway, with Gray still sipping from a rocks glass leaning against the wall next to her, shaking his head.

I knelt down beside her, and when I spotted what she'd discovered, all the breath wooshed out of me. It was my engagement ring—the real one.

"Chance!" I cried out, picking it up from the floor. "It's my ring!"

He came up beside me, but I was surprised when I turned to look at him that his lips were set in a hard line.

"What?" I shook my head in confusion.

His eyes shot to Zara. Whatever he wanted to say, he didn't want to say it in front of her.

I stood and showed the ring to Amanda, but was surprised when she and Hiram also seemed quiet and not happy like I thought they'd be. We'd found something.

"Why's everyone so quiet?" Zara asked. "This is good. We're close." She pointed to the door next to where she'd found the ring. "What's in that room? We should look in there."

"That's Ruth's room," Hiram stated, his voice monotone.

As if summoned, Ruth came walking up the back stairs, a stack of freshly laundered towels neatly stacked in her arms.

"What's all the yelling about?" Marcus asked, hot on her heels.

"Is everything okay?" Ruth asked, her eyes darting around to everyone gathered together.

"I—I need to search your room," Hiram told her, his tone and expression one of regret.

Ruth's lips parted, her disappointment evident, quickly replaced by resignation. "Of course," she said quietly. "It's your house."

Hiram took a hard swallow before stepping forward and opening the door, which I noted was unlocked.

Ruth's room was smaller than the guest rooms, but still outfitted with the same plush furniture that could be found throughout the rest of the house. I observed that the room felt rather spartan, with only a photo frame on the night-stand and a vase of fresh tulips next to the windowsill.

I wondered if it was that Ruth didn't have as many material possessions, or was so trained from having gone through the foster system that she didn't want to put roots down and get attached to any place. Maybe it was a bit of both.

But what really stood out in the room, was that smack-dab in the middle of the perfectly made bed, was a huge pile of jewelry—Amanda's jewelry.

Ruth went still at the door next to me. "That's not—I didn't —" she stuttered.

There was no way this was real. Whoever had actually stolen those jewels had dumped them on her bed. Even if she'd done it, wouldn't she at least hide them in a dresser drawer?

I leaned down next to Ruth, and taking a chance, I whispered, "Whatever happens next, just play along. Everything's going to be okay."

She looked up at me, her big brown eyes full of questioning and just the smallest bit of hope. I looked over at Hiram and was pleased to see he'd observed the interaction and understood what I'd done.

"I'm going to ask you to stay in your room until the storm has passed and we can get the police out here," Hiram told Ruth.

She bowed her head. "I'm sorry," she said simply.

"I told you it's always the help," Zara chimed in from next to the bed, shaking her head in smug vindication. "You should be ashamed of yourself," she sneered at Ruth.

"That's enough," Amanda growled.

I took the stack of towels from Ruth, who seemed to have gone into shock. I set them down on the dresser, taking one from the top over to the bed.

"Shouldn't we wait for the police to take photos or something?" Gray suggested.

Amanda came up beside me and looked at the pile. "This looks like most of it. I'll go through it and see if anything is missing."

Gently, the two of us transferred the pieces to the towel so we could more easily transport it back into her closet.

"I—I need to start dinner," Ruth spoke up from the corner of the room, where it looked like she was trying to disappear completely.

Zara loudly guffawed. "I don't want her anywhere near my food."

"She's a thief, not a poisoner," Marcus chimed in.

"I'll take care of the food," Hiram told everyone. "Ruth, just stay up here, out of the way, okay?" His tone was gentle and reproachful.

She nodded, her body curling into itself.

Having finished gathering the jewelry, I helped Amanda gently lift up the bundle. Hiram came alongside her and took it from her, despite the fact that it wasn't too heavy.

"Everyone out," he declared, leading the way out of the room and holding open the door until everyone was in the hall. He turned to regard Ruth. "I'll come talk to you later," he told her.

She nodded.

I flashed her a small smile before the door closed, cutting her off from the rest of us.

"What a relief," Zara declared.

"Rather anticlimactic, don't you think?" Marcus shrugged, already walking down the hallway back to his room.

"I know a prosecutor who could take care of things under the table," Gray told Hiram.

"I'm good," Hiram ground out. "The weather is supposed to clear overnight, so if we're lucky, the roads and power may be back up in the morning. I'll set out some food for dinner later, but otherwise you're on your own."

Zara and Gray frowned at the turn of events, but eventually followed Marcus down the hall toward the rest of the rooms.

"What did you want to say about the ring?" I turned to Chance, the piece still clutched tightly in my palm.

"It was in a ring box," he told me, his eyes bouncing to Amanda's, who nodded in agreement. "That ring was planted outside Ruth's door."

"I figured as much. Most jewelry thieves don't leave their entire hoard lying out in the open." I snorted.

"One of them set her up." Amanda was furious. "I swear to god, when we figure out who, I am going to eviscerate them for traumatizing that poor girl."

"I'll go talk to her." Hiram turned back toward the door. "Let her know it's okay." He paused, his eyes set firmly on Amanda. "You." He glared at her. "Back to bed, darling."

Amanda harumphed in protest, but turned and stomped off toward their room anyway.

Hiram extended his hand with the cache of jewels to Chance, who took it from him. "Make sure every last piece is there," he commanded.

12

CHANCE

"This feels silly to put all of this jewelry back into a broken safe," Amanda lamented. Hiram had pulled two chairs into the walk-in closet for Violet and Amanda to sit, while they worked together to dutifully disentangle all of the necklaces and bracelets from one another and slowly replaced them on their original displays.

"You can get a new one installed," I suggested handing her another piece, fiddling with the black velvet box in my pocket that Amanda had discreetly passed to me before they started parsing through the collection to make sure everything was returned. Violet had immediately traded her replica ring for the real one, but she didn't know about the custom wedding bands, safely tucked in the box.

"I'll have to figure out where we can move it to, because I'm not putting it back in the same place after this whole fiasco."

"Maybe the bathroom," Hiram suggested from the closet doorway, where he and I had been observing their little operation.

"So we all agree Ruth was set up, right?" Violet asked. My muse, always a little impatient to get back to the task at hand.

"I imagine it would have been quick enough to find her record, but just her position in the house would be enough for an outsider to assume she'd be an easy target to frame," I noted.

"I still wonder how premeditated this whole thing was." Violet paused in her detangling and stared at me. "Was the plan always to return the jewelry this quickly, or did our thief get scared and dump it, hoping there would be no repercussions?"

"And if it was always the plan to return everything this quickly, why?" I added. "What could they possibly have to gain from doing that with such a high risk of getting caught?"

"Don't forget, they couldn't have predicted the storm would trap us in the house," Amanda stated.

"When were the guests supposed to depart if the roads hadn't been washed out?" I asked.

"This afternoon," Hiram added.

I hummed in disapproval. "So we can't rule out that this could have been their plan all along. They would have had time to enact the same course of events, whether they were stuck or left on time."

"Surely you must have more insight on the three of them, Amanda," I commented. "You've been working with Marcus for months and even though you hadn't met Gray and Zara before this weekend, I know you did a deep dive on them in your circles before you'd let them step foot in your house. Originally I assumed there was a financial motive, although now that the jewelry was returned so quickly, that assumption could be called into question. What reason would any of them have to do it?"

"Marcus is a pussycat. He puts on a big show, but I think he really loved his wife. Yes, there was a big age gap, but he was a successful architect before they met, he just hadn't set up the firm yet. I never met her, but the way he talks of her is reverent, and I know people that knew them when she was still alive and said they had the best banter. Maybe they were more friends than lovers, but who are we to judge?" Amanda had paused in her task to face Hiram and me.

Violet's brow was furrowed, focused on detangling a particularly difficult snag in a necklace, but I knew she was listening intently.

"Let's walk through a world in which Marcus is the culprit. What would be his reasoning?" I pushed.

"It doesn't make sense." Amanda shook her head. "I don't believe Zara's gossip that his firm's on the verge of collapse, and if the office is being mismanaged, he could hire different staff. It's fixable, even if true. He's still got a great reputation, a star-studded client list, and frankly, his work speaks for itself." She gestured generally to the house around her. "He'd only have something to lose because his reputation is everything, and he knows that."

"What about the contested will?" Violet asked, her gaze still fixed on the necklace as she spoke. "If he lost the inheritance, where would that put him?"

"I guess he might have to scale back on some extravagances, he does have a taste for luxury, but he could also just take on a couple new clients to make up the difference," Amanda offered. "I've asked him why he keeps going—why he doesn't just retire—and he loves his work. I mean, you've met him." Amanda gave me a pointed look. "He loves people—loves women, loves feeling adored. He likes that he's so well regarded, and it was his career and his skill with design that's gotten him to where he is. His wife's rolodex just fast-tracked his likely success."

As much as Marcus irked me, Amanda was right. His motivations were practically transparent, and it didn't make any sense that he would have risked his future and livelihood. But

I couldn't deny there was something about how he'd reacted to the discovery at breakfast that wasn't sitting well with me. Maybe he wasn't the thief, but he knew the most about the safe, and I had a sneaking suspicion he knew more than he was letting on. But Amanda didn't want to hear it, so I'd have to discuss it with Violet later and see what she thought.

"What about our not-so-happily married couple?" Violet must have sensed the same thing I did, that the conversation about Marcus wasn't worth pursuing further at the moment. "They've been having a lot of verbal arguments in their short time here, witnessed by multiple people, including Chance and me."

"Ruth said it sounded like they were arguing about money when she heard them fighting in the gym the night before last," Hiram recounted.

"She told us the one thing she heard clearly was about 'all the money being gone,'" Violet repeated what Ruth had recounted earlier that morning.

"But what money?" Hiram asked. "It's obvious his current startup is on the cusp of crashing and burning."

"They might have even been talking about Zara," Amanda piped up.

All heads turned to her.

"One of the companies she shills supplements for got terrible press a few months ago for issues with a batch that made a ton of people sick and even hospitalized a few. Zara stood by them for much longer than she should have and only backed down when she was about to be canceled herself for putting a brand deal over empathy for the victims."

"Why do I have a feeling someone like her has a long list of scandals that have been swept under the rug?" Violet chided, clearly no love lost between her and the reality star-turned-entrepreneurial influencer.

"Because she does," Amanda agreed. "Insensitive remarks, shady business practices, and even her new venture, the wellness retreats, are starting to get some backlash when regular people pay exorbitant prices and don't get the A-lister treatment they're expecting, based on what other influencers have shared about their experiences."

"It sounds like both her and Gray are just grifting from one pyramid scheme to another." I crossed my arms over my chest, shaking my head in disgust. Swindling people out of money was abhorrent. I wasn't sure how they could sleep at night. "How much of their personal money do you think is tied up into the startup?" I asked Hiram.

"If they were smart, none of it, but Gray seems to think this is going to be his big break and put him up on a pedestal with the other tech greats, so who knows. Maybe he bet it all and is hoping the tides turn in his favor?"

"That would be incredibly shortsighted." Violet rolled her eyes.

"Does he strike you as someone who makes logical and well-researched business decisions?" Hiram half laughed.

"So what could they have to gain from the jewelry, other than the obvious cash flow, which still feels ridiculous because they'd have to know a fence that could sell the jewelry fast enough that they'd have the money for the business, but not so fast that it would be traced back to them," Violet spoke up.

"A fence?" I chuckled. "You've been watching too many heist movies again."

She stuck her tongue out at me.

"They also have a lot to lose," Amanda noted. "While it's not uncommon for a lot of these tech bros to go bankrupt, multiple times over, to keep chasing the next big thing, Zara's reputation would flounder, and one too many failed startups with huge investments would eventually catch up to Gray. If they were linked to a robbery, they'd be tanked. The circles we run in are miniscule and they'd be blacklisted so fast it would make your head spin."

"One of them has to be the mastermind." Hiram sighed, clearly growing tired of the endless conjecture.

"Marcus is smart enough, but has a weak motive. Gray is devious enough and has a strong motive. Zara strikes me as too self-obsessed and high-maintenance to have orchestrated this whole thing, but she has just as strong of a financial motive as Gray if their fates are linked together based on the outcome of his current startup."

"We're missing something." I shook my head. Something wasn't right. The puzzle pieces weren't fitting together. "What other connections have we overlooked?"

"I think Marcus might have fucked Zara." Violet giggled.

I raised a brow at the accusation and Amanda's lips parted in surprise.

"What?" She shrugged. "He made a comment about her mouth that struck me in a certain way. And she made a comment about Marcus knowing how to take care of a woman. Her tone was suggestive. I just got the sense that there was something more there."

"Ahh, that makes sense." Amanda nodded.

When the closet remained silent, waiting for her to elaborate, she continued. "I overheard them having a heated exchange in the hallway the morning before you both arrived." She motioned to me and Violet. "I went out there to see if everything was okay, but they'd stopped fighting and...well they were closer than I was expecting. I didn't see anything, but it was almost compromising."

"You didn't tell me that." Hiram scowled.

"I forgot." She frowned. "I was busy calling the chef to ask him to double his servings since Zara and Gray weaseled their way into staying another night, and preparing for their arrival." Again she pointed to me and Violet.

"Chance is right. We're missing something." Violet huffed, leaning back in her chair, the tangled necklace discarded on the island countertop. "What if money isn't the motive? Or it is, but it's a byproduct, not the primary directive?"

"You're right, Violet," I agreed. "Usually it's the most obvious answer. But sometimes it's not."

"Like what if Marcus and Zara were having an affair and they want to pin this on Gray so Zara can abscond with his money, or whatever's left of it and ride into the sunset with her flirty boy toy?" Violet threw out.

Amanda and I both stifled a laugh at her use of "boy toy" to describe Marcus.

"Maybe someone wanted Ruth out of the house?" Hiram suggested. "But I don't know why. I guess we'd have to find a new house manager if she wasn't here."

"What else?" I encouraged.

"Well, Zara and Gray were the ones who "found""—Violet used air quotes to emphasize the word—"the jewelry. Maybe they thought it would earn enough goodwill that you'd change your mind about investing?"

Silence fell over the room as a bunch of factors clicked into place.

"That's a hell of a lot of trouble to go to." Hiram sounded a bit skeptical.

"But it sounds like they might be just desperate enough to do something completely irrational to get what they want," Violet countered.

God she was hot when she was on a roll.

"If we follow that line of thinking, we need to consider that they were probably in on it all together," I said.

"We need to press Marcus for more information about Zara. If they really are hooking up, it could throw a wrench into our theory, and my gut says he knows something." Violet was resolute.

"I want answers," Amanda said quietly.

"And we'll do whatever we can to get them for you," I confirmed.

Thankfully the rest of the day passed without incident. Rain continued to pound the house, with wind rattling the windows. If you listened hard enough, you could even hear the rough ocean waters crashing violently against the rocky shoreline.

After the events earlier in the day, it seemed everyone was content to remain in their quarters. Even dinner was a droll affair, given the limited food that was on hand. Violet was happy to make the two of us sandwiches and eat them up in the room.

I loved how the simplest things made her so happy. When she practically flounced into the room, sandwiches in hand, and I asked what the cheerfulness was about, she said she was just happy to get to spend time alone with me. My heart fluttered in my chest at her adoration and earnestness.

She only ever wanted me. Nothing else. Just me. It seemed unfathomable.

"I should curse my mother for getting you that thing." I peered down at her, nestled in the crook of my shoulder where she was using the e-reader my mom had gotten her for Christmas.

Violet used it almost every night, which wouldn't have been a problem, except for the nights when she was so engrossed in her current read that I had to use all sorts of creative methods to tear her away from the pages.

"Do you really think the jewelry getting returned was strategic?" I asked, wanting to revisit the conversation.

"Yes," she stated plainly.

"Why?"

"Because they could have dumped the jewelry anywhere. But they chose to dump it in Ruth's room and pin it on her. There's malice there. There's intent. If they were scared, I think we would have just found it all out in the hallway, where it would lead to nobody. Hell, the fact that they tried to frame Ruth allowed us to firmly rule her out," Violet argued.

"Who's your best guess?" I goaded her. I loved hearing her brain working.

"Zara."

"Alone?"

"She could have roped Gray and Marcus in, or maybe both." Violet shrugged.

"Why Zara? She seems like such a flake. You really think she could do something like this?" I might have been intentionally winding Violet up, but I wanted her to really sell me on Zara. Although the jewelry had been discovered, I knew how determined she was to figure out who'd done it definitively.

"A flake?" she squawked, twisting in my arms and flinging the e-reader behind her as she leaned on one elbow over me. "She was on *Housewives* for three seasons. Do you know how cutthroat they are on that show?"

"Do you?" I laughed. "You don't watch it."

"No, but I know about it. You don't hold your own on a show like that for more than a season without being a decently conniving person. Zara may not appear to you like someone that can play 3D chess, but she can and does, just with emotions and favors, rather than rooks and pawns." She pointed a finger at my chest. "If Zara's hemorrhaging sponsors like Amanda alluded to, and Gray's company is on the verge of collapse, you bet your ass she's both smart and dumb enough to try something this ludicrous to gain favor with someone as influential as your sister."

"But we heard them arguing before we went down to dinner. Doesn't that narrow their window of opportunity?" I raised a brow, amused by her fervor. "Just because you don't like Zara, doesn't mean she did it."

"First of all"—she jabbed her finger into my chest—"I know you're just trying to wind me up, so I'm not going to reply to that last part."

I stifled a laugh, which had her rolling her eyes.

"Second, yes, that was in the middle of the half hour we've identified, but if they knew what they were doing, they wouldn't have needed to take very long. Third"—she held up three fingers, right in front of my eyes, to prove her point—"they very well could have been arguing about what they'd just done."

"You said 'they,' so you do think Gray was involved?"

"I still don't know." She shook her head. "But I have to admit, I find it hard to believe that she could have done all of this, from start to finish, without any help."

"It does feel a bit implausible," I agreed.

I took a beat to admire Violet. She was so fucking strong, and so fucking smart to have helped us get this far in our impromptu investigation. It might have even been her foresight to suggest that the thief could return the jewels that had resulted in them reappearing.

And to take the lead on something like this...it was brave. All I ever wanted to do was protect her, but I was starting to realize she didn't need my protection...in fact, she didn't need me at all. But she *did* want me. She'd chosen me. And that was more than enough.

"I want to talk to you about something," I said softly, pivoting from the robbery.

"Is everything okay?" she asked apprehensively.

I nodded. "I want to talk about the house."

Violet's shoulders slumped. "Do we have to?"

"No," I relented. "But I'm anxious about it, and I don't want to hide that from you."

Her expression softened. I was typically more of the go-with-the-flow kind of guy, especially in our relationship, so she understood if something was stressing me out, it was a bigger deal.

"Tell me," she whispered, reclaiming her spot in the crook of my shoulder.

"The landlord called again the day before we left. He's serious about selling the place," I confessed. "I'm worried if we don't buy it, it'll be sold out from under us and we'll be forced to move out."

Two lines formed between her brows as she gazed at me with concern. But she said nothing. And a quiet Violet was a dangerous one.

"I don't want to move, sweetheart. And I know you love the house. So let me buy it. Let me do this. For us," I pleaded.

Her eyes strayed from mine, and I just knew she was overthinking things.

"I know you're worried about things being equal between us. I'll do whatever it takes to make you feel comfortable—whatever kind of arrangement we need for you to contribute in a way that allows for you to feel like it's yours too."

That had been the sticking point when I'd brought it up before. She wasn't in a financial position to be able to pay for half of everything, especially not up front. But this was the perfect reason to dip into my trust fund for the first time, to set us up for the future and to ensure we could keep the house we both adored.

"I wouldn't want my name on the deed if you bought it," she said after a moment.

I frowned. That wasn't going to work. "It's important that your name's on the deed because of the prenup my Dad forced you to sign," I told her. "I need to make sure if anything happens to me that you're taken care of."

She gritted her teeth.

"Do you at least see where I'm coming from?" I asked softly. I needed us to be on the same page. This was too big of a decision. I couldn't make it without her. She had to be on board, or it was never going to work. I worried that whatever path forward we chose, if not forged correctly, could erode the beautiful and solid foundation we'd worked so hard to build with each other.

"I understand that I'm allowing my pride to override practicality." She sighed, her tone defeated. "I understand I don't have a choice."

"That's not true," I argued quietly. "If this is a deal-breaker for you, I can live with it. I know your reasons, I promise I do. But we need to be realistic that the consequence could be us having to find a new place to live."

"I know." She looked up at me with those big green eyes, tears beginning to well along the bottom rims. "There's a line in our relationship I don't want to cross when it comes to money," she explained. "I can't *ever* have you question why I'm with you—how much I love you."

"I know how much you love me, muse. I know if I was penniless, you'd still think I'd hung the moon. But I'm tired, Vi. I'm tired of fighting over every small bill, thinking you need to prove your worth and feelings for me at every turn.

"I've promised not to intervene with your student loans and your mother's mortgage, and I hope you know how hard it is for me to let that debt eat at you when I could wipe it all out in an instant. But I let it fester because I love you and I know you need to pay for it all yourself, if for nothing else than to prove to yourself that you can do it. But this house is for both of us. It's for *our* future—for the life we've been dreaming of building."

With eyes still glassy, she gave me a knowing look as she finally replied, "Okay."

"Just okay?" I leaned down to place soft kisses on her cheeks, then her lips. "I was hoping for something a little more enthusiastic." I nipped at her bottom lip, watching as her eyes flared at the intimacy and the current that was always running between us like an unbreakable thread.

"Then give me something to be enthusiastic about," she teased, smiling up at me.

"If buying you a house to show you how much I adore you doesn't get you off, then I don't know what will," I joked.

"You've never had a problem getting me off before." She bit her bottom lip, looking up at me through her lashes.

"No, I haven't, have I?" I grinned. "Let's take this off"—I tugged at the straps of her bra—"and I'll see what I can do."

13

VIOLET

"Just the man I wanted to see."

Marcus paused mid-sip as he regarded me cautiously upon my approach the next morning.

I recalled Amanda mentioning offhandedly the day before when we'd spoken of Marcus that he was an early riser, so I set my alarm extra early, leaving a sleeping Chance dozing in the bed to have some alone time with Marcus, hoping to coax some additional information out of him.

"Changed your tune, I see." He smirked, setting his coffee cup down next to a plate of toast.

"We'll see." I smiled, rounding the kitchen island to fix my own cup of coffee.

It appeared that at some point overnight the power had come back on, and I was back to having spotty reception, which was certainly better than nothing at all. While the ominous clouds of the early morning seemed like they might dump more precipitation at any moment, for the time being, it was holding off.

"I was hoping to speak with you about Zara." I leaned my elbows against the countertop, watching Marcus like a hawk.

He stilled at my statement and looked dare I say, nervous? The poor thing.

"Does Gray know about the affair?" I asked.

Marcus's eyes went wide and his head swung toward the main staircase. "Keep it the fuck down," he hissed.

Well, confirming that was much easier than I'd thought it would be.

"Worried Gray will overhear?" I grinned.

Marcus clenched his jaw. "What do you want?" he asked through his teeth.

I took my time pouring the hot water into the mug and mixing it with the instant coffee. I took slow steps across the kitchen to retrieve the creamer from the refrigerator and then to replace it. Gingerly, I paced over to him and slid into the dining banquette next to him. His eyes were fixed on me in a glare, angry and unnerved.

"I want to know how involved you were in the robbery." I looked him straight in the eyes, making my demands as clear as possible.

His nostrils flared as he exhaled, eyes widening ever so slightly.

"I wasn't," he sputtered.

I cocked my head at him. "Come now, Marcus." I tsked before taking a sip of my coffee. "You may not have been the one to nab the jewelry from the safe, but you *were* involved."

Did I have proof? Nope.

Was I certain that he'd either directly or indirectly provided information about the safe that had led to the theft? Yup.

When Marcus continued to stare at me, sweat beginning to bead at his brow, I pushed a little further. "You'd really risk your livelihood and potential jail time for *her*?"

"Jail time!?" He shook his head. "I didn't do anything, I swear."

"Marcus." I used a firm teacher voice to catch his attention.

His eyes snapped to mine.

"Tell me what happened and I'll make sure Amanda doesn't press charges or leak your involvement to her friends." They weren't exactly my promises to make, but he didn't know that.

"I didn't realize I was giving her information. I had no idea what she was up to! You have to believe me." He leaned forward, grabbing my arm to punctuate his innocence.

"I *do* believe you," I told him, although I certainly hadn't made my mind up yet. "But you have to tell me everything."

His eyes were frantic as they assessed me, trying to discern if I would be true to my word or if this was indeed a well-crafted trap. "I can't help that I like pretty things," he began. "And Zara is very beautiful in her own way. She's starved for attention. You think Gray is giving her what she needs?"

I didn't answer his rhetorical question.

"Did it start this week, or before?"

"I've seen her around town, and we'd spoken briefly at a party about her house design—"

"The one she can't afford?" After all, it was Marcus who had spilled those beans already.

"But it's not her fault. Gray put every penny she had into Atmosync without telling her. And then the cofounder ducked out when prototype testing went awry. Why do you think it's so important he gets funding? It's not just Gray's neck on the line, it's Zara's legacy," Marcus argued.

"It sounds like she's made a convert of you?" I replied dryly.

Marcus shook his head. “It was just supposed to be a bit of fun. Gray was wrapped up trying to convince Hiram to invest and Amanda wasn’t interested in giving Zara the time of day. So we kept each other company.”

“And that’s when she brought you in on her plan to steal Amanda’s jewelry?” I wanted answers, and I wanted them now.

“NO,” Marcus hissed, then his shoulders slumped. “But she did ask about the safe.”

I wasn’t able to avoid the interest in my expression.

Marcus sighed. “She was in a bit of denial about Gray having siphoned her funds for his business venture, so I humored her when she asked about it for her own house—the one she was convinced I would be building for her. It was foolish, but it just felt like pillow talk at the time.”

“But then the safe was looted.”

He nodded, the color draining from his face. “I didn’t think she was capable of something like that, but when everything mysteriously reappeared in Ruth’s room...” His gaze met mine. I wanted to believe the remorse I saw in his expression was genuine. “I knew it was her. She felt like Ruth wasn’t taking her requests seriously, and she’d expressed her frustration to me.”

"Tell me she didn't do this just to fuck over Ruth?" I half exclaimed.

"No..."

"But you know why?" I pressed him.

"Gray needed the investment. Zara wanted her money back. She thought Amanda would be so grateful they found the jewelry that they'd reconsider," he admitted, I could almost hear him realizing as he said it out loud how fucking stupid that plan sounded.

When I'd theorized that very motive with Chance the night before, I'd felt silly for suggesting something so ridiculous. But it would appear Zara's hubris was built on sheer audacity.

"Unbelievable." I shook my head. "But Chance and I heard Zara and Gray arguing in the room next to ours halfway through the window of opportunity. How did she manage to ransack the jewelry in just a few minutes?" I needed to make sure I had all my ducks in a row.

"I'm in the room next to yours," Marcus replied.

"What?"

"I'm well aware of how happily engaged you are. The walls aren't as thick as you'd expect, something I'll have to remedy on future projects," he teased.

I felt my face go beet red at the implication that he'd heard Chance and me having sex.

"*I* was fighting with Susan that night, before dinner. She'd secured a new lawyer and called to threaten me, hoping I'd give in and return her mother's money."

Just then, something clicked into place. "That's why she knew when the chef arrived, because her room overlooks the front drive at the far end of the hall. Your room would have a north-facing window."

Marcus nodded. "What did she want with the chef?"

"An alternate menu, but now I'm wondering if it was meant as a diversion or for her to somehow have an alibi for the general time period of the robbery," I speculated aloud.

"Maybe?"

"But there's one thing I still don't understand: they had the jewelry in hand. The collection is worth probably tens of millions, if not more, especially at auction. Why not sell the pieces, or even dismantle them for the diamonds and gemstones?" I had to ask, especially while Marcus was finally being honest with me.

"Optics," he replied simply. "Yes, selling the jewelry would have been much more difficult to recoup the money they wanted, but if they got Hiram to invest, not only would they have the immediate cash influx, which Zara was going to put back in her accounts, but Hiram is a well-respected venture capitalist. If he invests in something, people notice and follow suit. Gray could get the company fully funded within days," Marcus explained.

"But what happens when the tech inevitably failed to make it to market, because that's what it sounded like the outcome would be?" I noted.

"Gray would have long sold the company by then. He'd have his money and be on to the next startup." Marcus shrugged.

"You mean the next con." I rolled my eyes, disgusted with the things rich assholes were allowed to get away with.

"What are you going to do now?" Marcus asked hesitantly.

"I'm going to ask you to keep our conversation between us for just a little while. And when everyone is down here for breakfast..." I allowed a mischievous smile to unfurl. "I think I'd like to put on a little show."

Slowly, the rest of the group trickled in for breakfast. First were Amanda and Hiram, who were surprised to see me up so early, let alone without Chance at my side. But it gave me time to let them in on my plans.

Chance was next. My heart leapt when he shot Marcus a wary glare on his way to me. "Hey, baby," he murmured, tugging me into him as he dropped a kiss on the top of my head, his eyes never leaving Marcus.

"I made you coffee." I smiled up at him, pointing at the steaming mug on the counter next to mine.

"Thank you." He gave the back of my neck an affectionate squeeze.

And then the guests of honor arrived.

With all the fanfare I had come to expect from Zara, she floated down the stairs wearing a floor-length silk caftan with a blue-and-white print, complete with a matching giant blue sunhat in hand. "Good morning, darlings," she greeted all of us in the kitchen.

Grey trailed her in cuffed white slim-fit trousers, loafers with no socks, and another grey quarter zip, his eyes already glued to his phone.

"I like your dress." I smiled, luring her into a false sense of security and specifically not referring to the proper name of her garment, because I knew she'd correct me.

"Actually, it's a caftan."

My grin widened, pleased to have been proven correct.

"Dolce & Gabbana, vintage resort wear," she added, as if the label would impress me. Which it of course did not.

"It's a lovely day to make my flight to Ibiza—finally." She greedily snatched the mug of coffee Amanda had set on the counter before her. "Thank goodness the power and internet came back up. My followers were so relieved to hear that I'm alright."

Over in the entryway, I spotted Ruth, who had just finished lugging the guests' suitcases downstairs. It was funny how they so easily dismissed her until they needed "the help" for manual labor.

Amanda must have had a chance to tip her off because she tentatively paced toward the kitchen, stopping just where the entryway turned into the expansive shared space.

"I'm so glad we're all here," I decided to begin. "I've had a break in the case."

"But the jewelry was recovered," Gray piped up.

"It was, but we never discovered who had taken all of it in the first place." I stared at him.

"Of course we did," Zara chirped, leveling a glare at Ruth, who was still awkwardly positioned at the periphery of the room.

Ruth promptly withered under the attention, but Amanda was quick to slip over to her, placing a reassuring arm around her shoulder.

"You see, all of you are thieves in different ways, but only one of you robbed the safe," I told the group.

"How dare you. I'm no thief." Zara balked.

"Aren't you though?" I questioned, taking a few steps toward her. "This wellness guru grift has to get tiring after a while. Do you even test the products you so willingly sell to your followers? Those retreats you lead, how much do they cost regular people, and are they getting the same experience as the celebrities you host? Is that not theft?"

Zara's eyes blazed, but she said nothing.

"Lovely Marcus is a thief of hearts." I turned to him, watching him pale under the scrutiny, still unsure how much I planned to bring him into this debacle. "Collecting women like trophies, but leaving a trail of broken hearts in your wake."

"They come to me willingly," Marcus argued.

"I'm sure they do." I nodded, continuing to move through the space, narrowing my focus on my next target. "I wonder how much money you've stolen through the years, Gray?"

"Bitch," he sniped.

"Don't fucking talk to her like that," Chance snarled.

"She's a fucking liar," Gray bit back.

"Oh, but Gray, I think you've done enough lying for both of us. How many days do you have left before Atmosync collapses? Have you told your investors about how the tech doesn't work? I'm sure it won't take long for them to figure it out now that your cofounder has abandoned you. And it's no secret that this is one failed company in a long line. How many have you swindled and sold on a dream that you knew didn't or couldn't exist?"

His nostrils flared and jaw clenched, but he said nothing.

"You, too, are a thief," I stated, my eyes never wavering from him.

"Last, but certainly not least is, Ruth." I rounded on her. She took a step toward Amanda, perhaps misunderstanding my intent. "You all were so quick to throw her under the bus because she's not one of you. She doesn't own property or an investment portfolio. Does that really make her so worthless in your eyes?" I asked.

Nobody replied.

"Ruth is a thief as well." I spared her a soft glance. "But stealing groceries as a homeless teen isn't quite the same as fraud, is it? She may not have your wealth, but she has integrity and strength of character. Can you say the same for yourselves?"

"This is ridiculous," Gray muttered as he poured something from a flask into his coffee.

"You're right," I agreed with him.

He reared back.

I continued to pace, making my way back toward Zara, whose nervous gaze followed me.

"You must have thought it was so easy to get the information about the safe from Marcus," I told her.

Her brow knit in confusion, but the rest of her tense body language betrayed her.

"I wonder, did you program in the master override code before we arrived, or did you manage to do it the night you took the jewelry?"

"What!?" she squawked.

"It must have been devastating to find out that your own husband siphoned all the money you worked so hard to earn from duping your followers into buying useless snake oil, into his failing business." I circled her. "You argued in the gym about it the night before dinner. Had you already formed your plan by then, or was that when things started to come together?"

"This is ridiculous," she sputtered, looking around for someone to come to her rescue.

But no one said a word.

"You figured if Gray got Hiram to invest, you could get your money back, and if you were lucky, maybe a few more investors would hop on board and throw cash at him before the company tanked. You had to figure out how to get Hiram to invest when it was pretty clear he wasn't interested. But you know men well enough to recognize how devoted he is to his wife. Maybe you thought if you could gain some serious goodwill with Amanda, she and Hiram would be so grateful they'd change their minds," I relayed my theory.

It was Ruth who scoffed with disgust.

"So you devised a plan to take her heirloom jewelry, with the intention of returning it, but you'd make sure you'd be the one to find it. All's well that ends well. Because you assumed Amanda wouldn't care about anyone in her employ. I'm not even sure if you knew Ruth had a record, but she was a perfect patsy in your eyes."

Chance stifled a laugh, probably at my use of the word "patsy," but I was in a flow state. There was no stopping me now.

"You called down to the chef to demand a separate menu, trying to place yourself in your room, and give yourself an alibi—but honestly, it was shaky at best. You absconded with the jewelry after using the default master override code, and then waltzed into dinner as if nothing had happened. After that, it was just about finding the right time to dump the jewelry in Ruth's room and feign the discovery of the ring that had miraculously fallen out of the stash right outside her bedroom door."

Zara shook her head, face bright red.

"You must have been so disappointed when Amanda and Hiram stood by Ruth. But then again, you couldn't have known Hiram had grown up with her. He knew she would never do something after he gave her a job and a place to live, providing the stability and love she always needed when they were younger. You picked the wrong person to frame. Marcus would have been a much better choice."

Marcus sputtered, half choking on a sip of coffee when I brought him up.

"So tell me, what have I missed? I'll admit, I'm curious to know if you actually thought this would work or if you saw it for the long shot that it was? I'm also not sure if or when Gray knew you were involved, though I suppose it doesn't really matter, does it?" I shrugged.

"You are out of your mind!" Zara seethed.

"Zara, didn't do this." Gray shook his head, but it didn't sound like he was so convinced himself.

"Besides, you have no proof." Zara switched tactics, firmly planting her hands on her hips. "The jewelry was returned. There's nothing to be done."

"You're right." I shrugged.

The room stilled again, unsure of where I would go next.

"Nobody's called the police. The roads have reopened. So you're free to go." I motioned toward the entryway.

Zara eyed me skeptically, her gaze darting between me and the door, perhaps calculating her escape. "What's the catch?" she demanded shrewdly.

Hiram stepped forward to deliver her sentencing. "The catch is that we will not be proceeding with any investment, and I'll make damn sure nobody else puts money into whatever Ponzi schemes the two of you cook up next."

Gray balked at the accusation.

Then Amanda delivered the fatal blow. "Just because we haven't involved the police doesn't mean what you've done won't get around. You know how quickly word spreads in this town, and I don't think something this scandalous has happened in ages."

Zara's expression morphed into one of horror, realization sinking in that her life as she knew it was over.

"Ruth was nice enough to bring your luggage down for you." Amanda pointed to the roller bags by the front door. "So if you'd kindly get the fuck out of my house and never come back, it would be greatly appreciated."

Even when she was kicking someone out of her house, she

still managed to sound so even keeled and elegant. I envied her decorum in every situation.

Those of us remaining watched, myself with quite a bit of glee, as the pair struggled to move their luggage out to the driveway, arguing with each other as they loaded the bags into their car. I wasn't sure what would become of Zara Sable and Grayson Bennett, but I knew I'd be glad if I never saw or heard of them again in my life.

Marcus cleared his throat behind the group, and his eyes went wide when everyone turned to him. "I think it's best if I take my leave," he said quietly.

He grabbed for the handle of his luggage, but stopped short as he turned to Amanda. "I'm so sorry for everything," he told her softly. "I hope you know I had no idea something I considered a harmless conversation in the moment would result in such a dramatic outcome."

"I understand," she replied solemnly, not giving him the warmth she reserved for those she cared about...the warmth she once used to regard him with. "I wish you well, Marcus," she told him, perhaps assuaging his fears for his future.

Amanda didn't strike me as a vindictive person. After all, she knew, having grown up in East Coast, old-money society, that you never wanted to make enemies of anyone, but you did want to collect and use information to your benefit.

Amanda's relationship with Marcus would likely disintegrate, but she would allow him to live his life without fear of retribution, knowing he'd learned a very difficult lesson, at her expense.

"Are you alright?" Chance asked Amanda.

"I'm just glad it's over and that they're out of my house." She sighed in relief before turning to Ruth. "I'm so sorry for what they put you through. Hiram and I will always have your back. You will always have a place with us."

With tears in her eyes, Ruth reached out to squeeze Amanda's hand, then turned to repeat the gesture with Hiram. "Thank you."

"And I hope the two of you can finally relax for a few days, despite everything that's happened." Amanda smiled at Chance and me. "Thank you for figuring all of this out. I don't know what I would have done without you."

"I just wish I felt more vindicated." Chance sighed next to me. "They get to go back to their cushy lives. It's not fair after what they put you all through."

"They won't be punished by the court of law, but they'll have to deal with a fate far worse: the judgment and expulsion from their peers," I reminded him.

14

CHANCE

Violet's husky moans filled my ears as I slowly rolled my hips against hers, buried so deeply inside her I never wanted to leave.

Mornings that allowed for us to sleep in usually started with a nice, slow, round of morning sex. I hoped it would always be this way between us. Of course the sex was always amazing, but it was through our physical connection that we seemed to ascend to a new level of emotional intimacy as well. It was part of our own language. It was ours alone.

"Feels so good..." she groaned when I hit that spot she loved.

As I pressed closer, leaning down to suck at the fading hickey on her neck from a few nights previous, her legs clamped harder around my hips, pulling me against her.

"I thought you wanted it slow," I teased her.

"Changed my mind," she grumbled.

Always happy to follow her lead, I increased my speed and slipped my hand between us, finding her clit and gently circling it until she was panting and writhing beneath me.

With a sudden jerk of her hips against mine, she came, surprising even herself as she could only surrender to the pleasure. With a few more strokes, I followed suit, my hips snapping against hers as my release overwhelmed me. The sheer ecstasy never ceased to amaze me.

As Violet tucked her body against me, so comfortable that she fell asleep again almost immediately, all I could think was that she had no idea that today was our wedding day.

"Are you nervous?" Amanda asked me.

We were seated next to each other in the dining nook off the kitchen, watching the early morning sun casting its first rays across the ocean and beyond.

"Yes," I couldn't help but respond automatically.

"Why?" Amanda asked, her tone sincere. "You've taken all her wedding dreams into consideration. And we both know how much she adores you."

"I just want it to be perfect."

"It will be," Amanda argued. "But if it isn't, what are you worried will happen?"

I sighed, rubbing my hands down my face. "I don't want to disappoint her. She's going to remember this day for the rest of her life. I want it to be worthy of her."

Amanda leaned back in the banquette, nodding her head, as if she'd just had some huge epiphany.

"What?"

"You said you want the day to be worthy of her, but what you really mean is that *you* want to be worthy of her." She smiled, knowing she had me pegged.

"I don't ever want to be without her," I whispered, almost hoping Amanda hadn't heard me. The thought of losing Violet physically pained me. I feared doing anything that could lead to her changing her mind about me...about us. Because being together was a choice. I needed her to choose me, just like I'd chosen her, long ago.

"It's so disarmingly sweet how she's made you both soft and strong at the same time, but never small," Amanda commented. "Do you really think a woman like Violet would ever be with a man she wasn't obsessed with? She wants to be cherished and respected. You give her those things without a second thought. I promise you there's nothing to worry about."

I took a long hard look at Amanda as she regarded me. It had taken me so long to see that my sensitivity wasn't a weakness. Hell, Violet had told me before she considered it a strength, which made my chest warm and tight.

I needed to allow myself to be loved by her.

Because if I was good enough for Violet, that should be all that mattered.

"You'll have to wake up your sleeping beauty soon." Amanda smiled. "I've booked a full day of couple's spa treatments for the two of you, so you're out of the way while I make sure everything is set up for later."

"Set up?" I raised a brow "What are you setting up? We're supposed to just say our vows out on the back lawn at sunset." I had been clear it was meant to be as simple as possible. No fuss. No fanfare. And definitely no guests.

"I have some light florals coming in," Amanda began. "Light," she repeated when she saw my eyes widen. "I'm having another chef come over to take care of food for the day, and a photographer because I know you'll both regret it if you don't have any photos after. Not to mention Violet's hair and makeup."

"She won't want hair and makeup, Amanda." I glared at her.

"It's not like that." Amanda narrowed her gaze at me.

"Then tell me what it's like," I said through my teeth, hackles raised. We'd been discussing this for weeks. I'd extracted every last detail from Violet herself. If it wasn't exactly what she wanted—exactly as I'd communicated to my sister—there was no do-over.

"She's not getting full glam. Just gentle touches to make her feel a bit more elevated." Sensing my discord, Amanda reached out, her palm resting on my forearm. "I'd never make her look or feel like somebody she is not, not today." Her eyes bored into mine. "I just want her to feel pretty. I need you to trust me, Chance."

I puffed out a breath. I knew it was my nerves. I knew that. But it was hard to breathe through it. I wondered if that was what it was like all the time for Violet when she was working through her anxiety. "I trust you," I replied quietly.

Amanda flashed me a smile. "You're getting married today, big brother. Today is going to be a good day. I promise."

I felt my chest and shoulders loosen at her sentiment.

I'd be a husband within hours...tied to Violet forever.

I knew if I could just make it to sunset, everything would be okay.

VIOLET

"C'mere." Chance opened up his arms to me and I crawled into his lap, pressing my face into his neck to breathe him in.

We were situated on the back patio in big white fluffy robes, all soft and boneless after a couple's massage Amanda had arranged for us. She'd actually insisted on a full spa day, and that was just the last treatment we'd gotten. I'd never felt more relaxed in my life.

"Doing okay?" Chance asked before pressing a soft kiss to my forehead.

"I feel great." I smiled up at him. "I just wish Amanda would have let me paint my nails black instead of this sheer pink." I held out my hand in front of him to show him my nails.

"They look nice." He reached out to slip his fingers between mine.

We took a beat, just staring out at the ocean beyond the cliff-side, the waves crashing against the craggy shore below, basking in the late afternoon sun.

"Would you marry me tomorrow?" Chance asked. Our little joke, now so familiar, always made my heart skip a beat.

"I'd marry you today," I happily answered him without hesitation. Because it was the truth. Because I loved him more than I'd ever thought possible. Because he was my soulmate.

"Okay." He reached out, tucking a strand of hair behind my ear. "Let's get married today."

I chuckled against him.

"I'm serious." His fingers gently grazed my temple. "Let's get married today."

I sat up in his lap, my brow furrowed. "Today?"

"Today."

"But it's a Saturday."

"There's a notary arriving in two hours. Amanda has a dress for you upstairs." His blue-grey eyes were a storm of emotion as they searched mine for an answer.

A grin split my face. "Okay."

"Yeah?" Hope lit up his features. Did he think I'd deny him? I'd do anything for Chance.

"Yeah!" I shoved at him playfully. "Let's get married today!"

He laughed at my antics, the relief apparent on his face.

Amanda must have been watching, because she stepped out onto the patio at just the right moment. "Good to go?" she asked Chance, sporting a knowing smile.

"We're getting married today!" I cheered, planting a swift kiss on Chance's cheek before hopping up and grabbing Amanda's hand.

"I'll see you at sunset, muse," Chance called after us. But Amanda was already dragging me inside.

The next couple hours were a blur of champagne and hair and makeup. I felt like I was floating on air. I couldn't have cared less what Amanda's helpers did to me. I just wanted to get back to Chance.

"How are you feeling?" Amanda asked, leaning casually against the door of her bathroom, having just dismissed her glam squad, as she called them.

"I feel beautiful," I replied honestly, swallowing the lump in my throat as I regarded my reflection in the mirror.

When she'd first shoved me in the room with her helpers, I'd been reluctant. I didn't usually wear much makeup, and I was a teacher, so I was lucky I had enough time to wash my hair, let alone style it. Chance loved me for exactly who I was. I didn't think I needed anything special.

But they'd all assured me they wouldn't do anything drastic, and true to their word, I was left with the lightest hint of makeup, and gentle curls. The top half of my hair was pulled into a soft braid, with small pieces of baby's breath woven into the plait.

"Baby's breath is the perfect understated but modest flower for you, Violet," she'd told me as she helped the hair stylist place them throughout the braid. "It's so often overlooked, but it's the anchor to any timeless arrangement. The flower elevates others and is always so steadfast."

I felt my chest tighten at her words. She was always so thoughtful and considerate. I was so lucky to get to call her family.

"Plus, giving you violets felt way too on the nose, although they are pretty." She laughed.

Looking at how each stem was perfectly placed within my hair with such care made my heart swell. There was no detail forgotten.

"You ready for the dress?" She bit her bottom lip, practically shaking with excitement. I wondered how long this had been in the works. How long had she been waiting to show me?

I merely nodded, almost bursting with anticipation myself.

She ducked over to the closet, and only a moment later, appeared with the dress on the hanger.

I blinked back tears.

I knew the moment I saw it that it was mine. That Amanda had hand-selected this dress from god knows how many others, just for me. Other than the simple elegance of the garment, it wasn't close to any of Amanda's tastes, but it was perfect...for me.

Made of what I assumed to be silk, it was a simple slip dress, with a bias cut, allowing the fabric to flow and drape like liquid. With a simple V-neck and thin straps, it was just as Amanda had described the baby's breath: understated, but elegant nonetheless.

But what really made the dress special, was that instead of a traditional veil, hanging over the silk was a translucent chiffon cape. I wasn't sure if I could pull it off, but boy was it beautiful.

Because of the simple design, it only took me a moment to slip it on. Of course it fit like a dream, and the cape...there were no words. I felt like a princess. Although I didn't dare tell Amanda that, or I worried she'd insist on a tiara.

"No jewelry?" I questioned, one brow raised skeptically.

"Not today." She smiled softly. "You already have the earrings and necklace from Chance, and Grandma Mitzi's ring." She glanced down at my heirloom art deco alexandrite engagement ring. "You don't need anything fancy to be the most perfect bride for my brother."

"Amanda..." My voice wobbled. "I'll never be able to thank you...for everything."

"You don't need to thank me." She reached out, squeezing my hand in hers. "The way you love my brother is more than enough."

I blinked back the tears welling in my eyes.

"Don't cry." She dabbed at my eyes. "You'll ruin your makeup, darling."

I huffed a laugh.

"Are you ready to get married?" she asked me quietly.

"I'm ready." I'd never been more sure about anything in my life.

We took our time walking down the stairs, careful of the dress and cape flowing behind me, although she'd been kind enough to put me in flats, probably so I wouldn't sink into the lawn the moment I left the tiled patio.

"You look stunning, Violet," Hiram greeted us at the bottom of the stairs.

"Thank you." I felt my heartbeat increasing at the thought of getting to see him again. "Where is he?"

"Just outside," Amanda answered me. "I'll escort you, if that's okay."

I nodded quickly, suddenly feeling nervous butterflies erupt in my stomach.

I never imagined any of this. For years, I shut myself away from everyone else, so heartbroken from those who had come before. Even when I met Chance, I spent months pushing him away. But he never relented. He gave me my space. But he continued to show up. It all felt like a dream.

A shutter clicked to my left and I started.

"Don't mind her," Amanda whispered, politely acknowledging the photographer. "I just wanted to make sure you had something to remember this day."

"Okay." I swallowed, my breath suddenly hard to find.

But the moment Hiram opened the door to the patio and I spotted Chance waiting on the back lawn, framed by the sun setting over the ocean, it was as if the rest of the world melted away, and there was only him.

Standing primly, his hands clasped in front of him, he wore my favorite charcoal suit, with the blue-grey tie I loved, which matched his eyes. He beamed at me so brightly his smile crinkled the corners of his eyes, and I thought I might die from happiness.

Amanda held me closely as we walked down the fabric aisle that had been laid between the end of the patio and my groom.

When we finally made it to Chance, Amanda gently took the small bouquet of baby's breath from my hands and gave my arm a reassuring squeeze. Then she turned to Chance and pushed up on her tiptoes to kiss him on the cheek. "We'll be inside when you're finished."

We both watched as she made her way back into the house and when we were alone again, the air charged around us, Chance finally broke his silence. "You are a vision."

I couldn't help but laugh. It was probably nerves, but I didn't think I was nervous. I was just ready.

Chance reached out to wipe away tears I hadn't realized were falling down my cheeks. "I hope I got it right." He cupped my cheek in his palm, tilting my head to look up at him. "Just us. By the ocean."

"The charcoal suit." I smiled, tugging at his blue-grey tie. "It's perfect." I blinked back more tears. "*You're* perfect."

And it was perfect.

He'd listened to me. Every word.

Everything I'd ever mentioned about the wedding, how I'd wanted it to be intimate and romantic and something that felt like us and not what everyone else thought we should do. He'd done it.

I allowed myself a moment to take everything in, the ocean waves a constant metronome against the shore, the salty ocean breeze making my sheer cape billow behind me in the wind, Chance's rosy cheeks in the chill of twilight, and how the warmth and orange light of the setting sun cast the most beautiful haze over the pair of us.

I looked up to meet Chance's eyes, glassy with unshed tears as he regarded me. He was breathtaking. Nobody had ever or would ever look at me the way he was in that moment, with such reverence.

He'd put all of this together just for me...for us.

"Amanda says we can say our vows and the notary will sign the license inside," he explained.

"Don't we need a witness?" I wasn't sure how any of this worked.

"They'll make an exception. So we can be alone," he replied. "Just us."

"Just us," I repeated. That's what I'd told him over and over again. That I wanted a wedding that was just for the two of us.

"Can I go first?" he asked, his voice apprehensive.

"Are you nervous?" I half laughed. My Chance was always so confident. That couldn't be right.

He merely blushed in response. My stomach swooped.

I reached between us and grabbed his hands with mine. "You've already done the hard part," I assured him.

His eyes met mine.

"You won me over a long time ago."

He chuckled. "Somewhere between us getting stuck in a coat closet together and snowed in at a highway motel."

"No, it was before that." I shook my head, my lips curled. "It was when you drove me home after you saved me at the bar."

He raised a brow, intrigued by my answer.

"The way you talked about your photography—and you were so curious about me." I laughed. "I suppose you did suspect me of being a criminal at the time, but still."

We burst out into laughter together.

"You go." I squeezed his hands. "I'll listen."

Chance took a deep breath and squared his shoulders before finding my gaze again, and then he began.

"I think I always knew, from the moment I saw you, that you were mine. I didn't know you then, but I felt it. I think you did too."

I smiled up at him. I had felt it too.

"But you weren't ready yet. You needed time. So I gave you time. You needed space. So I gave you space. You needed someone to fight for you. So I fought for you." He paused. "I will *always* fight for you."

I blinked back tears.

"It's crazy that this thing between us always felt inevitable, but it did. I wasn't going to give up. I wasn't going to let you go. I couldn't. I still can't. Every piece of you brings me to life. Watching you try every day to be a better person than the day before is nothing short of a miracle. Some days I don't feel worthy of you—"

I couldn't help but scoff, submitting to the tears streaming down my face, which he again reached out to wipe away.

"But I've realized you've chosen me. And if nothing else, I trust you. I trust you with my heart, my life, my future. I'll choose you every day, if you'll let me. I'll love you to the end of my days and into the beyond. I can't wait to spend the rest of my life with you, my beautiful, brilliant muse."

His shoulders slumped in relief, as if saying all of those things out loud had been weighing on him so heavily. As if he hadn't shown me every day how fiercely he loved me.

"How am I supposed to follow that up?" I sniffled through a laugh.

He cracked a smile.

"You should have let me go first." I pouted.

His smile deepened.

"You always know the right thing to say." I looked up, finding his eyes fixed on me with such warmth and intensity, any nerves I had evaporated. "It's been in the small moments that I've fallen in love with you so deeply. You'd think I'd be upset about drowning in it, but instead I bask in it. I've never felt more seen or heard than when I'm with you. And the way you see me..."

I shook my head, still in disbelief at the man standing before me. "You say I'm strong, but every ounce of courage I have is from you. I was so sad...so lost before I met you."

He squeezed my hands in comfort.

My eyes met his again. "I think maybe I was just waiting for you. I think I was just waiting for you to come along and fill in all the cracks and missing pieces and put me back together. You've given me the support I never realized I was missing, the words of adoration I didn't know I needed, and the unconditional love I hadn't understood had been absent."

Then it was my turn to reach out and wipe away a tear as it rolled down Chance's cheek.

"You make me want things, and need you, and dream. You've made me feel, finally, that I am enough. And you are too." I caressed his jaw.

"You are everything," I whispered, repeating the words he'd said to me once. I hadn't believed them then, but he'd painstakingly proven to me the truth in them day after day.

Unable to bear the distance between us any longer, Chance leaned down, pulling my face to his as he kissed me softly and sweetly, sealing our vows.

When we finally needed a moment to catch our breaths, Chance pulled back, and reaching into his pocket, he pulled out a black velvet box, popping it open to reveal two simple gold rings, one slim with a curvature that would perfectly fit against the shape of my engagement ring, and the other slightly thicker.

He held his hand out for mine, slipping the slim band on my finger, nestling it against his grandmother's ring, and then offered me the box, allowing me to place the thicker band on his finger.

"No takesies-backsies." I giggled up at him.

Without warning, he pulled me into a much more heated kiss, whispering into my mouth, "Never."

EPILOGUE

VIOLET

A small piece of paper hit the whiteboard next to where I was writing out my notes for the next day's class.

"You better pick that up." I snorted, glancing at the wad of paper at my feet with derision.

The desk behind me groaned as Chance stood from his perch to bend down and pick up the paper, only to throw it at the back of my head.

I spun around and chucked my marker at his face, which he annoyingly anticipated, catching it with one hand while reaching out and grabbing my wrist with the other, yanking me to him.

"I'm busy," I whined as he slipped his arms around my waist, pulling me closer.

"You write too slow," he whispered, trailing soft kisses along my neck.

"You're making me slow." I pushed against him half-heartedly.

"The headmistress is making her rounds," Chef Lenny called from the doorway. "Better be careful."

"Thanks, Chef." I pushed Chance again, but he wouldn't budge.

"We're married now, she can't do anything!" Chance called after him.

Lenny merely shrugged and grumbled as he readjusted his bag over his shoulder and continued toward the faculty parking lot to leave for the day.

Despite his eternally grumpy disposition, Lenny had been thrilled when I'd shown up to school a month prior, with Chance in tow, sporting our shiny new wedding bands.

Hell, even the headmistress had failed to hide a smile when we'd shared the news. I'd always known she was a closet romantic. She'd had cause to let both of us go after she'd discovered our relationship the previous year, but instead had chosen to let us continue on at the school and with each other, as long as we kept things discreet.

"I need to finish." I glared up at Chance.

"You're procrastinating," he accused me.

I clenched my jaw, a retort on the tip of my tongue. But he was right. I sighed in defeat, my shoulders slumping.

I turned to look at my half-finished notes on the same whiteboard Chance had pinned me against last year, begging me for understanding, wanting desperately to be in my good graces.

"Come along, wife." He smiled, tugging on the hem of my cardigan. "Let's go home."

"Don't tell me what to do." I stuck my tongue out at him, but I was already packing up my bag.

Before I could grab it, Chance snagged the bag and slung it over his shoulder, then took my hand, pulling me out of the room. "I'm going, I'm going," I groused. "No need to be early for the inquisition."

"My mother adores you." Chance squeezed my hand as we made our way to the car. "You don't have anything to worry about."

"She's never been to the house before. It needs to be perfect," I worried.

"It is perfect. We've been cleaning for days."

"What if Toby bites her?"

Chance stopped us on the front stairs. "Toby is harmless. It's going to be okay." He leaned forward, cupping my cheek as he kissed me sweetly, a frequent distraction tactic.

Which unfortunately always worked.

"No kissing on school property," I chided.

Chance laughed. "You know that's not a real rule."

It had only been a few days since we'd closed on the house, and it still didn't feel real.

Thankfully, there hadn't been any issues with the inspections and with everyone, including our landlord, quite motivated, I was surprised with the speed at which it all moved. Chance of course refused my request to not be listed on the deed, but we'd come to an agreement about how I could financially contribute over time, to earn back the equity in the house I felt it necessary to provide.

But I would have been lying if I said the whole situation hadn't made me realize that I was being too stubborn about the whole thing, and that while my heart was in the right place, I was keeping track of all these small things, which was the very thing I was trying to prevent Chance from doing. It was a vicious cycle and one I was still working through with Dr. Short in therapy.

"You've already dusted that bookshelf three times this week." Chance came up behind me and gently plucked the duster from my hand. "Everything's going to be okay."

I pushed my bottom lip out in a pout. I didn't care that I'd cleaned it already. I wanted to clean it again.

"Let's go take Toby for a walk and the lasagna will be almost done by the time we come back."

Upon hearing the word "walk," Toby came bounding over from his bed, where he had been observing my frantic dusting in peaceful oblivion, because nothing fazed our adorable little rescue pup.

As usual, Chance's instincts were right and I felt better after taking a quick stroll around the neighborhood we could permanently call home. We moved around each other in the kitchen as if our steps were choreographed, when really we were just that in sync with each other.

Thankfully, all the food came out flawlessly, and at exactly seven on the dot, the doorbell rang, signaling Cindy's arrival.

She was dressed in a well-tailored navy suit, with a baby-blue charmeuse blouse that perfectly complemented her shoulder-length blonde hair and startling blue-grey eyes that Chance had inherited from her.

"Well, aren't you two a sight for sore eyes!" she exclaimed, opening up her arms and pulling us both into a hug at the same time. "All grown up and married." She planted a kiss on my cheek. "And a bonus daughter to boot."

I blushed at the praise, my heart stuttering as she pulled me into her tightly. There was nothing better than a mother's hug.

Not one to be left out, Toby pranced on his hind legs, begging for attention.

Cindy released Chance and me and bent down to regard our little dog. "You are so cute, I could just eat you up!" She laughed before picking him up in one swift movement and cradling him in her arms like a baby, allowing him easier access to lick her face, which only seemed to delight her more.

"Hopefully the drive wasn't too bad." Chance made small talk while he hung up her coat.

"Not at all." She smiled. "The house is even more charming than you told me," Cindy gushed. "Can I get a tour?"

And just like that, all my nerves and days of anticipatory anxiety slipped away. I'd forgotten how charismatic Chance's mother could be, and of course she was, that was where he'd gotten his natural charm from after all.

"We were worried you might be upset both of your children ran off and eloped," Chance joked over dinner.

"I raised you and Amanda to be independent thinkers and to do what was right for you," Cindy reasoned, taking a sip of her wine. "Of course I would have loved to be there, but I've seen the gorgeous photos, and knowing how happy all of you are is all that I want. But of course you'll have to tell me everything, and Amanda mentioned a jewel heist, but she was in a rush so she didn't elaborate, the little rascal."

For the next thirty minutes, over dessert, Chance and I regaled Cindy with the story of our spring break gone awry, in great detail, to which she was horrified. I'd even seen in the news in just the last week that Gray's business had collapsed, and there was speculation previous investors would join forces to press charges for fraud.

Zara hadn't gotten away unscathed either. She'd been dropped by most of the major brands she represented, and her supplement company was tanking amidst allegations of improper manufacturing and refining of the ingredients.

Perhaps everything that befell the pair had been inevitable, but I wouldn't have been surprised to find out that Amanda and her network of socialites had had something to do with speeding up the process. Karma was indeed a bitch.

"And then you return to Maine, married, and buy this gorgeous house." Cindy beamed. "Quite the happily ever after."

"We were lucky our landlord was willing to sell." Chance squeezed my hand on top of the table.

"I'm proud of both of you." Cindy's smile was so sincere I swallowed back the lump in my throat. She turned to me. "Did he tell you I tried to buy it for you?"

"What?" I turned to Chance, who was shaking his head.

"Don't worry. He wouldn't let me." She smiled, taking another sip of her wine. "We had a long talk about how important it was for the two of you to buy it together. I'm glad you found a compromise."

"Me too," I agreed.

"He also mentioned you've discussed some potential future renovations." She noted cheerfully.

"Well I think he needs a proper photography studio instead of having to jerry-rig his setup around the washer and dryer closet because that's the only place large enough without a window." I glanced at him. His photography made him so happy and if this was going to be our forever home, he needed a place to do what he loved.

"And if I'm getting a photography studio someday, then it only feels right that Violet gets her dream library," Chance added.

"With a rolling ladder," I told Cindy.

"With a rolling ladder," Chance agreed.

Cindy laughed.

Chance and I had had a lot of late-night conversations about our hopes and dreams for the house and what it could be, and those two rooms felt like a good start.

"Well, since you mentioned it." Cindy rooted around in her purse, pulling out an envelope and placing it on the dining room table. "While Chance said I wasn't allowed to buy you the house as a wedding gift, he didn't mention anything about not helping with your future renovations."

Chance and I shared a questioning look.

Cindy slid the envelope across the table to me.

"I hope you don't mind. I took the liberty of opening up a shared trust in both of your names to help fund those beautiful dreams of yours." She inched the envelope closer to me.

I stared down at it, then back up at her.

"I am so thankful every day that the two of you found each other. It's been such an honor to watch the love between you blossom into what it is today. Please let me be a part of building your future together," she pleaded, her eyes soft and her tone tentative, knowing this wasn't easy for me to accept.

And I did hesitate for a moment, but if nothing else, I'd learned from Chance that our love didn't require a ledger.

While Chance's background was different from my own, we shared the same dreams and goals. He only ever wanted to protect and provide for me. I knew he wouldn't use material things against me like others had before. I knew he wouldn't hurt me like that.

This gift from his mother was in good faith and without strings attached. Cindy loved generously, with her entire heart. Accepting her gift was the same as accepting her love.

I understood that now.

And so, with tear-filled eyes, I reached out and took the envelope, clutching it to my chest with a watery thank-you as Chance slung his arm around my shoulders, pulling me into him and expressing his gratitude to his mother as well.

Toby snoozed between us, his little pink tongue poking out. I knew there was no way he'd end up sleeping in the living room tonight, and I didn't mind.

Chance traced patterns on my bare shoulder while I talked through potential color options for my future library. "We could go classic with dark wood paneling, but I'm not sure that it matches the aesthetic of the house. How would you feel about navy or dark teal? Amanda mentioned this technique called color drenching where you even paint the doors and window trim the same color. I already started a mood board."

Chance snorted a laugh.

I glanced up at him where he gazed at me dreamily.

"What? You don't like it?"

"I love it." He smiled.

"Why'd you laugh?"

"Because you're adorable, and I'll paint the library any color you want."

"Even black?" I perked up.

"Even black." He leaned forward, kissing the tip of my nose.

I wasn't actually considering black, but I liked knowing he'd support whatever I chose.

As I watched his lips trail over my shoulder where his fingers had just been, it suddenly struck me that although I'd been lucky enough to grow up with a roof over my head, with a mother who tried so hard to love and provide for me, despite the hand she was dealt, that I'd never truly felt what it was like to have a home before.

This.

This was what it felt like to have a home.

And all the books and movies were so right.

Home wasn't a place.

It was a state of being.

It was a moment in time, where you truly felt as though you belonged.

And in that moment, in Chance's arms, with our little dog, in our cozy house, I realized something so profound it brought tears to my eyes.

I was finally home.

THANK YOU

Thank you for reading *Violet Among Thieves*!

If you enjoyed the book, it would mean the world to me if you would consider leaving a rating or review on Amazon, Goodreads, or the platform of your choice.

♡aj

Want more Chance & Violet? Visit **AJWynn.com/bonus** or scan the QR code to read a spicy bonus scene!

ACKNOWLEDGEMENTS

It wasn't initially my intention to revisit Chance and Violet, but it became apparent to me while promoting *Last Chance Christmas* and hearing from readers who loved it and wanted more of this fun couple, that their story wasn't quite over yet. And so Violet Among Thieves was born.

I knew immediately what this final installment of this unintentional series would be, and exactly how it would end. Reading their vows still makes me cry. I was surprised to find that although *Last Chance Christmas* was a breeze to write, compared to other books I've worked on, this book took much longer. And I have to wonder if it wasn't the fact that this was going to be the end for them that made me hesitant to complete it.

Regardless, as with all my other stories, it was indeed a village that helped to make this book happen. I would love to extend a huge thank you to all the amazing people that contributed to the production of this book from start to finish, including Heather, LL, and Kristin, my faithful beta readers, Sam, my phenomenal copy editor, Emarie my brilliant proofreader, and Rachel my unbelievably talented cover designer.

I was fortunate to work with both new and old artists on this book that all blew me away with their beautiful interpretations of this gorgeous couple. I also want to thank the ladies of Heartbound Bookshop, Natasha at The Well Red Damsel, and Stephanie of The Fleuria, who have all been so kind to share my books with their readers. And finally a huge thank you to my fantastic PA Sarah, who is always game for anything and only knows how to go above and beyond.

As sad as I am to say farewell to Chance and Violet, I know it's only goodbye for now, because I'm already thinking about ways to weave them into future stories. You never know who you'll run into in the halls of Montgomery Prep...

Thank you for reading. I am forever grateful for the love and support I've found in this lovely romance reader community.

See you in the next one!

♡aj

ALSO BY AJ WYNN

Willowbrooke

The Other Side

Last Chance Christmas

Radiant Exception

ABOUT THE AUTHOR

AJ Wynn is a Southern California-based author who works in marketing professionally, but whose true passion lies in writing. Weaving captivating stories with romance, mystery, fantasy, and much more allows AJ to express her creativity and serves as a canvas for her boundless imagination. When not immersed in the world of words, AJ is an avid reader, book dragon, and interior decorating enthusiast. Her favorite cozy days are accompanied by a fresh cup of coffee and her faithful canine sidekick.

To stay up to date on the latest news and releases, subscribe to her newsletter at **AJWynn.com** or follow on social media:

instagram.com/ajwynnwrites
threads.com/@ajwynnwrites
tiktok.com/@ajwynnwrites

Made in the USA
Coppell, TX
03 July 2026

84019873R00130